ONE KNIGHT STAND

MIDNIGHT EMPIRE: THE TOWER, BOOK 4

ANNABEL CHASE

RED PALM PRESS LLC

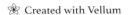 Created with Vellum

1

"**S**traighten your shoulders. You're too hunched. The universe has to feel your confidence. You need to set your intention and then follow through."

Sitting cross-legged inside the chalk circle, I squared my shoulders and prepared to try again. "I practiced this for hours yesterday."

"And you'll practice it again every day this week until you've perfected it." My mother stooped over the chalk circle to look me in the eye. "You are a very special girl, London. The upside of that is you've been blessed with many gifts. The downside is you have to work harder than everybody you know to control them so they don't control you."

"What's the point of all these gifts if I have to hide them?" I sulked.

"You want to live, don't you?"

I glared at her. "If I'm in so much danger because of what I am, why give birth to me at all?"

She booped my nose. "Because you are the living embodiment of love, young lady."

"Sounds selfish to me."

She resumed an upright position. "Perhaps it was, but the decision was made and here you are." She squeezed my left shoulder. "Now try again, London. Try as though your life depends on it—because one day it just might."

I concentrated on the black spot in my mind. My mother had noticed signs of a summoning ability and wanted to test her theory. She'd explained the power and how it worked. I was eager to try because portals and alternate planes sounded fascinating. My mother's reasoning was more practical. She thought it might provide a safe space for me to hide where no one could reach me. A panic room for emergencies until the threat passed.

I strained until it felt like every bone in my body might break. The effort was too much. Blood trickled from my left nostril and I collapsed on my side. I struggled to stay conscious, but my body betrayed me.

A firm hand shook me awake. "Time to try again, London."

I groaned. "No. No more."

"There's always more, my sweet. More to learn. More to master. If you think life is hard now, wait until you're older."

I opened my eyes and fixed them on her. Although I'd been raised in a world of darkness, as far as I was concerned, the sun rose and set on Rhea Hayes.

"Time to get up," she said, this time more firmly. "Now."

I opened my eyes and stared at the high ceiling.

It was time to get up.

I rolled off the mattress and stood to stretch. Just because I was a prisoner didn't mean I curled into a ball and gave up. I was keeping myself sharp, seeking out opportunities to overtake my captors and escape. Even without magic, I was strong, fast, and—most importantly—resourceful.

My mother had trained me well. If she didn't personally possess an ability, she either researched it or found someone who did. That someone had to be discreet and also willing to train a child who shouldn't be able to do the advanced level of magic that required expert assistance.

A child who shouldn't exist.

Despite her understanding of the world, my mother couldn't have foreseen that I'd one day be imprisoned in a tower in the castle of House Duncan courtesy of King Glendon. A tower that was designed to be a magic-free zone for prisoners like me.

I thought back to my lessons and tried to pinpoint one that might aid my escape. The 'panic room' later became the 'holiday home' for the menagerie, the group of animals that shared my flat. As I was the only one who could access the pocket dimension, it now served as the hiding place for two of the world's most powerful stones—the Elemental Stone and the Transcendence Stone. Unfortunately I couldn't access my safe space from here. No magic meant no portal to another plane of existence.

Try as I might, I came up empty.

This wasn't my first experience with captivity. Growing up in the tunnels beneath Britannia City had been its own kind of confinement. Hell, just being a dhampir in a world where vampires rule was a type of imprisonment. I'd constructed a metaphorical tower that kept me in and, consequently, kept everybody else out. Each day I woke up and lived a life where I concealed my true self.

I lived a lie.

Then again, the alternative was death.

The upside of my current situation was that I didn't have to worry about my magic imploding or exploding—there'd be no 'ploding of any kind. No silver glow of my skin. No stress over whether I'd eked out enough magic to relieve some of the pressure.

A low rumble shook the stones of the tower.

"Good morning," I yelled to the dragon.

There were no windows here that allowed me to see it, but I recognized the beat of its wing. The dragon flew past my prison every few hours. The first few days the sound would take me by surprise. Eventually I identified a pattern and could anticipate the dragon's arrival. This one seemed to be a creature of habit. If nothing else, the exercise kept my brain occupied which helped me maintain my sanity.

The dragon was the only thing I could count on. My captor attempted to use inconsistency as a torture device. I didn't know when my next meal would come. I couldn't anticipate the timing of a security sweep or which guards would be on duty. It suggested that King Glendon had a lot of experience with prisoners. I hadn't seen the king once since our conversation in the dining hall where he'd ordered his men to take me to the tower. Whatever his plan was, it didn't include communication with me.

I dropped to the floor for a dozen push-ups. I hated push-ups, but I needed to keep my body ready for action. I pictured Kami standing over me and giving me a hard time about my form. *Flat back. Move your hands down an inch.*

Lowering myself to the floor, I exhaled, wondering whether the king had found Callan. My guess was no, given the fact that I was still in here. At the very least the king would've paraded me around like a prize, maybe poked a few holes in me for good measure so that Callan knew I was viewed as expendable.

The king would be in for a shock when Callan showed disinterest in my fate. The vampire prince had told me as much when he abandoned me on the Isle of Skye. He'd learned the truth about my species and left me to my fate. Nice guy.

I finished the push-ups and went straight into squats.

Better not to take any breaks until the end of the set or I'd be tempted to feel sorry for myself. I allotted five minutes each day for a pity party and that was it.

A knock on the door interrupted my squats. A knock didn't necessarily mean a visitor. Sometimes they knocked and failed to enter, or they entered without knocking. The vampires were hitting me with their own brand of chaos magic. They seemed to enjoy it, too. I'd hear them laughing as they wandered away from the door.

"Who is it?" I called. I still played along, if only for my own amusement.

"Are you decent?" a high-pitched voice asked. He sounded like he hadn't hit puberty yet.

"Do you think I hang around the tower in my underwear?"

The door opened and two guards marched into the room with a third vampire behind them. I forgot to look to see which one sported acne. I was too busy staring at King Glendon. The waves of the vampire's reddish-blond hair were slicked back, revealing a few strands of silver. He looked dapper in a three-piece suit with a white shirt and a red handkerchief folded in his pocket. His long stride reminded me of Callan's and I reminded myself that the Highland king was nothing like his son.

The king flicked his wrist. "Leave us."

I caught a whiff of brandy on his breath. It seemed the king had taken a nip of liquid courage before he ascended the spiral staircase. Good to know.

The guards exited and closed the door, although I had no doubt they lurked outside.

"How's that plan working out for you?" I asked.

The king was unamused. "Are we treating you well?"

"Other than locking me in a tower and depriving me of magic, sure. Peachy keen."

The king observed me coolly. "You show me very little respect."

"Because you've earned very little."

His eyebrows drew together. "There's a hungry dragon outside these walls. You realize I could kill you right now and no one would ever know, not even my son."

"I think he'd put the puzzle pieces together. He's pretty smart. Apparently King Casek was adamant that Callan be given the same educational opportunities as his own children. He's treated him like a second son from the start."

The king flinched. "I think you mean *Prince* Callan."

"Correct. He is a prince. Gold star."

The king stepped forward and backhanded me across the face. "That's for your impertinence."

I bit my tongue and noticed a metallic taste in my mouth. Once I recovered from the shock, I straightened to face him. "If you want my cooperation, this isn't the way to get it."

"I neither want nor need your cooperation. I'll get what I want through my own methods."

"Then why are you here? If you came to leave a mint on my pillow, this is probably a good time to let you know I don't have a pillow." I motioned to the mattress.

"We've found that pillows have a way of becoming weapons, so we've had to make do without them."

"I don't think you're the one making do."

I thought he might whack me again.

"Tell me about the stones."

"They're hard pieces of earth used in the construction of buildings and even towers used to hold prisoners."

He didn't smile. "My spies tell me you've handled three

stones now. That makes you the world's foremost authority on them."

"They're not as big as I expected."

He clasped his hands behind his back and studied me. "You and I would make a formidable team."

"And here I've been under the impression that you're a solo player."

That prompted an amused smile. "I'd be willing to extend an olive branch for the right partner."

"Because you don't have access to magic?"

"Oh, I have plenty of access to magic." He gestured toward the door. "An entire team of witches and wizards at my disposal, in fact. I believe you've already met a few of them."

"Then why do you need me?"

He pinned me with those green eyes that were so reminiscent of his son's. "As I said, you are the foremost expert and I only like to partner with the best."

"Is that why you haven't remarried since your wife's death? Couldn't find a decent replacement?"

He regarded me with interest. "Why? Submitting your application?"

"I wouldn't bother. A vampire like you has no interest in building an empire with a witch as his queen."

"It is, in fact, forbidden here to marry outside the species, but I would have other uses for a woman of your many talents."

And the creep factor just cranked up to an unprecedented level. "We're still talking about the stones, right?"

He maintained his casual air. "Of course."

I folded my arms. "If you want to know about the stones, you might as well kill me because I'm not telling you anything."

"A pity." He started for the door and cast a glance over his shoulder. "Last chance."

I feigned interest in my fingernails.

"Thought as much." He knocked on the door and one of the guards opened it. "Bring in Sigmund."

Was I supposed to quake in my boots at a name like Sigmund? Titan, maybe. A Jericho could arguably be intimidating. But Sigmund?

It didn't take long for the torture device to arrive. I expected a wizard and a wizard was what I got. He was remarkably short, with brown hair so thin, I could see patches of pale skin on his head. He didn't wear a cloak. No, not our Sigmund. The wizard opted for a kilt and bagpipes.

I waved. "You can save the oxygen. I happen to be a fan of bagpipes, so your special brand of torture won't work on me."

Sigmund smiled. "Oh, the bagpipes aren't for you, love."

"No? Just the kilt?"

"Aren't you going to ask me what I'm wearing underneath? The ladies from other Houses always want to know."

"I have a special someone, so not really interested." Well, I thought I had a special someone. I brushed the thought aside. Now wasn't the time to think of Callan. I'd already used those five minutes earlier today.

Sigmund raised the bagpipes to his lips and blew. The first few notes sounded as expected. I folded my arms to show him just how unimpressed I was.

Then the shrieking began.

A translucent form pushed its way out of a pipe, followed by another.

Banshees.

They flew around me, screeching their taunts. The words were indecipherable, but the sound was intensely painful. Most people spoke to be understood. Banshees spoke to be heard in the worst possible way.

"I thought this was a magic-free tower," I shouted.

"This isn't magic, love," he called back. "They're banshees. Spirits like them can fit wherever they like." He patted the instrument. "Turns out they like the pipes. It's sort of like crating a dog."

More spirits emerged from the pipes, their screeches mingling with their predecessors. My eardrums felt like they were about to burst.

"Tell me about the stones," Sigmund said over the din.

I resisted. It would take more than this to break me. A lot more.

"You won't be able to hear me properly," I said. "Seems like a foolish way to extract information."

He beamed at me. "I'm fine. I've developed an immunity to their sound. One of the reasons my services are in such high demand."

Five banshees circled me. Their screams seemed to penetrate my brain. I dropped to my knees and covered my ears, but there was no blocking the horrific sound.

The door flew open. A cloaked figure hurried into the room and immediately closed the door behind them.

The king must've decided to send someone else to oversee Sigmund's handiwork. I didn't blame him for not doing his own dirty work. That staircase was a bear to climb.

Sigmund, however, seemed startled by the entrance.

The figure's hood slipped back and I recognized the witch from the dining hall, the one who'd 'prepped' me for my imprisonment in the tower.

"Cynthia, what are you doing here?" Sigmund demanded.

Maybe there was an expiration date on her magical mojo and it was time for my second dose.

"The king sent me to assist you."

Sigmund turned back to blow on the bagpipes again. Cynthia withdrew an object from the deep recesses of her cloak. I tried to see what it was, but my eyes kept closing against my will, as though that would somehow drown out the noise of the banshees.

The next time I opened my eyes, the banshees were still there, but Sigmund was facedown on the floor. My gaze flicked to Cynthia, who held a brick in her hand. She ran straight through the circle of banshees to reach me.

I stared at her in confusion. "Did the king ask you to do that?"

"No." She removed my confiscated weapons from the folds of her cloak and tossed over my beloved axe. "I'm here to help you escape."

2

"I n that case, shouldn't you have left the door open?" I nodded toward the door with no handle.

"We can't go that way."

"We're in a tower. What other way is there?"

I winced as the banshees continued to fly around the room like pigeons trapped in a dome. At least they couldn't attack us physically. A banshee's only weapon was her voice.

"Can you do anything about the noise? My ears are about to fall off." And with the way I felt right now, good riddance to them.

"We need the noise to cover our tracks. That's why I chose this moment." She raised her hands and the sleeves of her cloak slid down to reveal aging hands that contrasted sharply with her smooth features.

"What are you doing?"

She ignored me.

"Why are you helping me?"

"There will be time for questions later. Right now we need to hurry."

On the floor Sigmund stirred.

Cynthia's eyes rounded. "New plan."

"Already? I hadn't heard the first one yet."

The banshees returned to us and decided to make a nuisance of themselves at closer range.

"If you can pop off the lid to my magic, I can help," I said.

"My way is faster. The moment you leave the tower, you'll be able to access your magic. The spell on you only works in tandem with the tower's enchantment."

A faint light emanated from her hands.

"You can do magic in here because you haven't been 'prepped,'" I said.

"Correct. The enchantment of the tower alone isn't enough. There has to be a certain spell done on the prisoner that connects them to the tower. My spell."

I fell silent to let her work. Oddly, so did the banshees. They stopped shrieking and flew back into the bagpipes. It only took a moment to realize why.

Footsteps thundered up the spiral staircase. I listened to the fall of their boots and tried to count the number of guards. Too many.

Cynthia walked alongside the curved wall, dragging her hand along the stones. Magic sparked from her fingertips. I had no idea what she was doing.

Fists beat the door. "Open up!"

I glanced at Cynthia. "Now doesn't seem like the best time to file your nails..."

She stopped midway around the tower and formed a glowing green fist, which she then used to punch straight through the stone. "Go!"

I stared at the gaping hole. "Go where? We're like five hundred feet off the ground."

Then I heard the familiar sound of beating wings as they

approached the tower. I ran to the hole and peered outside.

The dragon flew into view, or as I liked to call it—my getaway car.

I climbed into the hole and prepared to mount my steed.

The dragon flew closer.

The door burst open and guards spilled into the room.

I jumped.

Cynthia's face was framed by the rubble. Behind her Sigmund rose to his feet. She couldn't stay or she'd be killed.

I extended a hand. "Come on!"

Her face was frozen in fear.

"Climb out! I'll get you!"

She turned and blasted her attackers with the same green light she used to punch the hole.

I steered the dragon back to the tower for one more pass, maneuvering us close enough to give Cynthia her best chance for a successful leap.

"Now!"

Cynthia took a flying leap. Her hands slid down the dragon's side and I gripped her wrist. It took every ounce of strength I had to stay balanced and pull Cynthia to sit astride the dragon at the same time.

The witch slumped behind me.

"Hold on to me," I told her.

Away we flew.

I attempted to win over the dragon but quickly realized it wasn't necessary. The dragon seemed willing to help without my magical influence.

"And here I thought you were their hungry second layer of security," I said, stroking the side of the dragon's neck. This wouldn't be the first time a dragon's actions had been misunderstood and it wouldn't surprise me at all to learn that the king and his staff never bothered to identify the dragon's needs.

"Careful," Cynthia warned. "It breathes fire. Prefers its meals roasted rather than raw."

"I'll be sure to stay on the safe side of his mouth."

"He?"

"This dragon is male." Even though I didn't convert him, I could still sense his very essence.

The dragon continued to climb higher in the sky. The air chilled my face, but it felt good to be outdoors again. To be free.

It wasn't easy to identify the right direction to go, mostly because I didn't know where the castle was located. If I were heading straight to House Lewis territory, I would simply nudge the dragon south. But I couldn't leave Scotland without the Spirit Stone and that meant finding Fenella. If the witch had done what I asked, then the stone should be hidden somewhere for safekeeping until I could arrive to claim it. Then again, Fenella had betrayed me once, which was the reason I ended up imprisoned in the tower in the first place. She and Murdina, both Shades with the Daughters of Persephone, had given Glendon's minions my location. Callan had left me on Skye, otherwise he would've been there, too.

I promised myself I wouldn't think about Callan.

The wind was strong, but the dragon cut through it like a knife through melted butter. I spotted a clearing up ahead and directed the dragon to land.

"What are you doing?" Cynthia asked, still clinging to me like her life depended on it. Fair enough, I guess.

"We need to regroup."

She didn't argue. The dragon skimmed the treetops and

landed in the open space. We were far enough away from the castle now that we could afford the detour.

The landing was bumpier than expected and Cynthia nearly got tossed onto the dragon's spiked tail, but we managed to arrive safely on land.

Cynthia wobbled to her feet, rubbing her backside. "Not as smooth as a broomstick, I'll tell you that much."

"Then you should've brought one with you to the tower." I glanced around the clearing. "We can use the dragon to help us make a small fire. If you see anything edible, give me a shout."

Cynthia scanned the clearing. "Are you certain it makes sense to stop?"

"Yes."

She seemed experienced at taking orders because once again she didn't argue. She simply went on the hunt for food. I created a fire bed with a ring of rocks and pieces of wood and directed the dragon to set it ablaze. I dragged over a section of a fallen tree and positioned it in front of the fire as a seat for us.

Cynthia returned to the clearing with the folds of her cloak in her hands. She arrived at the campfire and dumped a bunch of red and dark purple berries at our feet.

She joined me on the log. "Is a fire wise? Won't that attract unwanted visitors?"

"It's only the king's scouts I'm worried about and we've bought ourselves a little time." I cast her a sidelong glance as I rubbed my hands together in front of the flames. "How long have you worked for the king?"

"Decades too long. I started off in the pit and worked my way up."

I frowned. "The pit?"

"Not an actual pit. It's what we call the main group of

witches and wizards on staff. They're the lowest in the household hierarchy. Every witch wants to be elevated to the point where she's given orders by the king directly."

"Better wages?"

She nodded. "Job security, too. I never once saw the king when I worked in the pit though. He only deals directly with staff higher up in the chain."

"Did you know the queen?"

Cynthia's eyes glistened. "The queen was different. She made sure to learn our names, even staff in the pit. A fine woman with a sweet nature."

"Why would she marry someone like Glendon?"

Cynthia's laughter sounded harsh to my ears. "You think she had a choice? She was a gorgeous vampire from a powerful family with a voice like a nightingale. Her parents basically sold her to the highest bidder."

"But not from another House."

Cynthia shook her head. "The king didn't trust the other Houses. He was convinced that a bride from another House would plunge a dagger into his back while he slept and take over the realm."

It seemed like Glendon and Britannia had been cut from the same paranoid vampire cloth. No wonder they went to war with each other. They were too alike to co-exist.

"I think he was projecting," I said. "Glendon is the one who would kill anyone that stood in his way if it meant more power." I thought of the story Callan told me about his mother. Not who would kill. Who *has* killed.

"There's as much blood on his fangs as pumps through his veins," Cynthia agreed. "He's a monster."

"Is that why you decided to become a traitor?"

She jerked toward me. "I've been waiting for an opportunity to leave, but I knew I wouldn't be able to stay in Scotland. I expect you'll be returning to House Lewis. I wish to seek asylum there."

Any port in a storm, it seemed.

"Tell me more about the queen."

"She was the heart and soul of the castle." Cynthia's face darkened. "The castle changed after her death. The king was no different, of course, but everyone else seemed altered somehow. She was a ray of sunshine in this dark world. An odd way to describe a vampire, I realize, but that she was."

"And Callan?"

She cut a sideways glance at me. "The princeling? What about him?"

I laughed at the notion of the six-foot-four powerhouse of a vampire as a princeling. "That princeling is over thirty years old."

"Bah. He's nothing more than a vampire bairn. Tell me when you see a streak of silver and then maybe we'll refer to him as middle-aged." She stabbed a stick in the ground. "A proud lad. Tried his best to please the king but that's a Sisyphean task and everyone except him knew it." She clucked her tongue. "I always reckoned he was better off with House Lewis."

"What do you know about the Daughters of Persephone?"

Her lips curved upward. "I'm not one of them, if that's what you're asking. I may work for vampires, but I don't get my rocks off with any of them."

"I need to find one of the Shades. Fenella." I couldn't go to the sanctuary. That traitor Murdina would be more than happy to alert the king to my whereabouts, as she'd already proven. I didn't necessarily trust Fenella either, but if she'd done as instructed and hidden the Spirit Stone, then maybe there was still hope for her.

Cynthia looked crushed. "Why do you need Fenella? I don't advise lingering here any longer than necessary. Go straight home where you'll be safe."

I bit back a laugh. She had no idea how absurd that statement was.

"It's necessary, believe me. Fenella has something that belongs to me." Okay, technically the Spirit Stone didn't belong to me, but I was willing to apply the 'finders keepers' rule in this instance.

"You can't trust the Shades."

"I already learned that lesson, but I appreciate the warning."

The fire crackled and Cynthia gazed at the flames. "I'll accompany you."

"You don't have to do that."

Cynthia turned to face me. "I told you I want to seek asylum. Besides, there's much I need to atone for. Helping you is a good start."

On the one hand, sneaking two of us across the border would be more of a challenge. On the other hand, Cynthia was a skilled witch with inside knowledge of House Duncan. It seemed wiser to take her with me than leave her behind.

"I can direct you to the palace once we get to the city, but I can't go with you." After all we'd been through together, I wanted desperately to believe Callan wouldn't have told his family about me, but I couldn't stake my life on it.

Cynthia's eyes sparked with curiosity. "Not in good stead with the royal family there, are we?"

"I could ask you the same question."

She laughed. "Not after today. I held no sway with the king anyway. I did his bidding. Nothing more."

"I did save the life of Princess Davina. They like me for

that." I couldn't reveal any more than that without saying too much.

"A knight who saved a princess. A lovely story."

If only she knew the rest.

"Can I ask you something? Why do you keep your face from aging but nothing else?" Wrinkled faces were signs of a long life and people were usually proud to display them.

She gazed at the flames. "The king prefers youthful faces. In order for a woman to work in the castle, you must agree to look a certain way." She wore a wry smile. "As a vampire, he doesn't subscribe to the idea of an aging beauty." She finished the last of the berries. "I reckon we should keep moving. The king's scouts will be searching for us."

"First we need to find Fenella."

I took what my best friend Kami dubbed as the 'little birdie told me' approach. I used my connection with animals to pass a message around the forest that I was looking for Fenella. I started with a robin and eventually a blue jay appeared in the clearing to take the lead.

I motioned for Cynthia to mount the dragon. "It's go time."

"We're meant to follow a blue jay?"

"All the way to happiness, I hope."

"That's a bluebird."

I climbed on the dragon's back and pointed to the blue jay. "Follow his lead."

The bird took to the skies and the dragon followed. There wasn't much to see from above. The land appeared mostly dark from this distance.

Finally the blue jay started his descent and the dragon searched for space to land. The woods were too dense here, so he flew until he found enough room to lower himself to the ground.

The blue jay chirped and we trailed behind the bird until we arrived at a cottage in the woods. The building was made of white stucco with a thatched roof. Black shutters bordered the windows and a rustic red door beckoned us. I thanked the blue jay and he flew away.

Before we reached the welcome mat, the front door opened and Fenella stood on the threshold with her hands planted on her hips.

"Do I even want to know?" she asked. Her gaze darted to Cynthia. "I know you."

"This is Cynthia. Cynthia, this is the witch that stabbed me in the back."

Fenella held out a hand. "Fenella."

"You seem remarkably unconcerned for a woman who betrayed a knight," I said.

Fenella ushered us inside. "I knew you'd find me sooner or later given our last encounter. I suppose you'll be wanting what you left behind."

"That would be helpful, yes."

"One minute." She wiped her hands on her dress and disappeared into a back room. She emerged a few minutes later with the stone wrapped in golden chains.

I glanced at the doorway from where she emerged. "Where did you hide it? Your underwear drawer?"

"Best not to ask. Even with the anti-magic chains, I can sense its power. That's never happened before. I suggest you keep them on or you'll be going mad." She handed the stone to me. "I'm almost relieved to be rid of it."

"Thank you," I said.

Fenella bowed her head. "I'm sorry for turning you over to him. I felt like I had no choice." Her gaze drifted to the stone. "I couldn't see the bigger picture."

"You didn't know the bigger picture."

Cynthia raised a hand. "I still don't know the bigger picture."

"The less you know, the safer you are," I said.

Fenella frowned. "Will you give the stone to House Lewis?"

"No, I have other plans for it." *It makes a lovely scratching post for my cat in a secret pocket dimension.*

"Where on earth will you keep a stone so powerful that it's kept covered in anti-magic chains?" Cynthia asked.

"Somewhere safe." That was the most I was willing to reveal even to my rescuer. One answer would lead to another and next you thing you know, all my secrets would be tumbling out. I couldn't risk it.

Fenella's cheeks colored. "If you see Prince Callan..." She shook her head. "He was so distraught when I saw him again. I nearly confessed everything, but I didn't dare incur his wrath. If he's developed his father's temper, I didn't want to learn the hard way."

Cynthia nodded. "The Terror of Terra. Isn't that what they call him in your realm?"

The world around me seemed to slow to a stop. "You saw Callan again?"

"Aye. He arrived on the mainland after you'd been hauled away. I told him I was there to check on you, that there'd been a report of an arrest in the area and I was concerned." Fenella shook her head. "He was so distressed."

"Does the king know you saw Callan?"

Fenella chewed her lip. "That was a bridge too far for me. I adore that vampire. You, on the other hand, I could spare." She paused. "No offense."

An image of Callan's tortured expression flashed in my mind. "Did you confirm I was the one arrested?"

"And send him right into his father's arms? What do you

take me for? The king will have to do the rest of the legwork himself."

Then Callan must've left Scotland and returned to the city.

Without me.

As glad as I was that he'd avoided his father's snare, I felt as though he'd abandoned me all over again. Not that I didn't deserve it. I'd hidden a painful truth from him after everything he'd shared with me.

"What is it, child?" Fenella asked.

My head snapped to attention. "Nothing. I'm just deciding on the next course of action."

"Whatever it is, it best involve leaving this territory," Cynthia said. "The realm will be crawling with scouts before long."

I hugged the stone to my chest. "Ready when you are."

Fenella glanced from me to Cynthia. "You're going together?"

I stayed silent. Cynthia's plan wasn't mine to share.

"I'm going to help this one across the border," Cynthia said. It didn't escape my notice that she failed to include herself in that statement.

"I'd offer to help as well, but it's too big of a risk," Fenella said. "The best I can offer is to send any scouts in the wrong direction."

I nodded. "Good enough."

Fenella grabbed my arm. "If you see Callan again, please ask for his forgiveness."

My heart skipped a beat. "For me?"

She blinked. "For me, of course. Why would he need to forgive you? It isn't your fault you were captured."

"I'll tell him," I said.

I didn't bother to tell her that seeing him again was a pretty big 'if.'

"Would you like to stay for a meal?" Fenella asked. "I don't have much, but it's the least I can do."

"We need to keep moving, but thank you. Besides, you've already done the most important thing." I held up the stone. "This single stone is enough to start a war between Houses."

"Nobody wants that except perhaps the king," Fenella said. "The Houses will be fine. It's the rest of us who'll suffer."

"I worked on the front lines for a couple years," Cynthia said. "I promise you nobody there wants to fight..."

She left the rest of the statement dangling, but I filled in the blanks—*nobody there wants to fight on behalf of vampires.* It was treason to say the words aloud. Then again, the witches had already committed treason by helping me.

"At least take a warm cloak." Fenella retrieved a dark blue cloak from a stand and placed it on my shoulders. "Fits you well enough."

I slid my arms through the sleeves and thanked her.

Fenella released a reluctant sigh. "If there's nothing else I can do..."

An idea percolated as I placed the stone in the deep pocket of the cloak. It dragged the material closer to the ground. I'd have to walk lopsided.

"Actually, there is one more thing. May I borrow a few candles, a lighter, and a piece of chalk?"

Fenella laughed. "Keep them. I don't expect you'll be bringing them back anytime soon."

"I'd rather travel light. I'll use them outside right now and give them back before we go."

Cynthia's brow creased. "A cloaking spell?"

"No." I didn't need a cloaking spell when I could turn

invisible. "Just a healing spell for me." I offered a reassuring smile.

"I didn't realize you were hurt," Cynthia said, as Fenella disappeared into an adjacent room.

"Nothing major, but you'll want me in mint condition in case we meet any resistance on the way."

Cynthia assessed me. "Fair enough."

Fenella returned with a wicker basket containing the requested items. "You're welcome to perform the spell in my room."

"Thanks, but outside is better." I turned and left the cottage, making sure to close the door behind me. If anyone tried to follow, I'd hear them.

I hurried through the dark woods away from the cottage. Once I'd traveled a reasonable distance, I checked over my shoulder one last time.

I was alone.

I drew a circle with chalk and set up the squat candles. One by one, I lit them and then settled in the circle's center with the Spirit Stone in the folds of the cloak. The witches couldn't know about my summoning abilities. Fenella had betrayed me once. I couldn't be certain she wouldn't do it again with more valuable information.

It had been years since I accessed the alternate plane from anywhere other than my flat. I had everything I needed though. There was no reason for it not to work. With three out of five of the ancient stones, the holiday home I'd created for the menagerie was about to become the most powerful pocket dimension in existence.

I connected to my magic and focused. Reaching out with my mind, I searched for the portal. I felt its familiar energy and sighed with relief. Still there. I sent the Spirit Stone across time and space and closed the metaphorical door. As long as no one knew about my ability, they'd never guess the location of the stones and no locator spell on earth could find them. Even if someone attempted to torture me for the location, they'd need me to access the small realm. Because it was a place of my own creation, only I was capable of turning the magic key.

I opened my eyes and listened to the sound of the wind that served as background noise to the beating of my heart. A sharp breeze blew through the circle and extinguished the candles.

"Fine. I was done anyway," I said.

I dusted off my hands and gathered the candles. The air stilled. I lifted the basket of items and listened again. Footsteps?

My fingers tightened around the handle as I peered at the surrounding trees. If anyone tried to jump me, they'd end up with a mouth full of wicker.

I saw a flash of movement out of the corner of my eye and a white hart stag stepped into view.

"You're a good omen," I said. According to my mother, the white hart stag was known for its ability to evade capture, at least in the legends of King Arthur. I chose to take his appearance as a sign.

The stag's ears flickered.

"I'm glad we can agree on that."

The creature continued through the trees and I watched until only a speck of white remained visible. Then I turned and headed back to the cottage.

Cynthia and Fenella were waiting for me outside the front door.

"All set?" Cynthia asked.

"Yes." I returned the basket to Fenella. "Thank you for not stabbing me in the back this time."

"We should go," Cynthia advised. "I felt a shift in energy while you were gone and I don't know how to interpret it. Could be Glendon's men."

"If it is, I'll hold them off." Fenella stood on her tiptoes to peck me on the cheek. "I wish you a blessed journey."

Nothing about this journey had been blessed so far, but the appearance of the white hart stag strengthened the one feeling I'd nearly lost in the tower—hope.

We returned to the dragon and I was relieved he'd decided to wait for us. I hadn't commandeered his mind so his next move was anybody's guess.

"Where's the stone?" Cynthia asked.

"In my cloak pocket," I lied.

"And what does it do again?"

"I'm not sure exactly. I think it's meant to influence certain types of magic like mind control and telepathy." Although Cynthia's questions were reasonable, I had no intention of answering them truthfully. The fewer people who knew about the stones, the safer they were—both the stones and the people.

She eyed my cloak pocket. "Huh. You'd think I could sense it given my own abilities, but I don't feel anything."

"It's because of the anti-magic chains. I kept them on." I would've done that even if I'd kept the stone with me. Last time it trigged mind-reading abilities and I'd been forced to ask Callan to cloak his thoughts.

I quickly changed the subject. "Where's our best point of entry, do you think?"

"I've heard the king talk about Kelso being the weakest area of our defensive line close to the border," Cynthia offered. "Stands to reason that House Lewis might know this, too, and provide less defense there as a result."

"Worth a shot." I shared our plan with the dragon. He snorted two small flames in response.

Cynthia grunted. "I take it you've done this sort of thing before."

"I've ridden a few dragons," I said, nonchalant.

"I wasn't talking about the dragon, although that's pretty impressive. I'm talking about sneaking into foreign territories undetected."

I smothered the flames. "I've had help."

"It never occurred to me to try to cross the border on my own and throw myself on their mercy. I suppose I should've tried that years ago."

"I can't promise that would've been a happy ending for you. Hadrian's Wall is House Lewis's most heavily defended area. I doubt they would've trusted the word of a witch from House Duncan."

"That was my thinking as well. So how do we do this?"

It turned out to be surprisingly easy to evade House Duncan's border patrol in Kelso. Then again, it was really House Lewis that worried about another attack from the north. Bypassing their defensive measures would be the real challenge. There were a few layers of security but Hadrian's Wall provided the lion's share of protection. King Casek had even offered me a position there after I'd rescued Davina from her kidnapper. I'd turned it down, of course. The best way to keep my secret was to keep my distance from vampires.

That plan was clearly working well for me.

I craned my neck to talk to Cynthia. "I see lights ahead. Must be House Lewis border patrol."

"All right then. I'll provide a distraction."

"How? We're riding the same dragon."

Cynthia squared her shoulders. "I vowed to help you cross safely and that's what I intend to do."

"And I vowed to help you gain asylum."

"Tell your friend to take a steep dive, then climb high and fast, straight across the border."

"I'd like to know more first."

"Just do it."

I whispered our plan in the dragon's ear.

"Now!" Cynthia cried.

The dragon turned his nose toward the earth.

Cynthia swung a leg over the dragon.

"Cynthia!"

"Atonement, remember?" She surrounded herself in green light and jumped. She floated down like Mary Poppins with her umbrella.

I watched in horror as beams of golden magic streaked toward her on her way to the ground.

She lifted her chin for one last look at me. "Go!"

I went.

Her magical light drew the attention of the borderland defenses and the dragon and I sailed across under the cover of darkness. I felt like I couldn't breathe. I rode the dragon until I felt his wings grow weary. I couldn't force him to keep going. It wasn't fair.

I cast a glance over my shoulder as we landed. It was too much to hope for, but I forced myself to look all the same.

There was no sign of the witch.

I made my way to an overland train and carried on to Britannia City alone. For reasons I didn't understand, Cynthia had sacrificed herself to get me safely across the border and I refused to squander it.

There was still one more stone to find and no time to waste.

3

I had mixed emotions as I disembarked the train in Britannia City. It was my home, yes, but it was also my prison. The place where I'd lost my mother, but also the place where I'd created a family unit of my own.

And the place where the vampire side of my family still lived.

Now that I was finally here, the question was—where to next? I couldn't return to my flat. No doubt Prince Maeron had vampires watching the building. Those guys definitely drew the short straw. There wasn't much in the way of entertainment on my block. The other occupants of the building were pretty boring and kept to themselves, which was one of the reasons the flat suited me. I was also able to shelter more animals than was technically allowed by the bylaws. Occasionally someone complained about strange noises from above or the odd smell but, for the most part, the menagerie and I were able to avoid drawing attention.

I walked the familiar city streets to Covent Garden, sticking to the alleyways and circumventing the lights. I wasn't foolish enough to march into the headquarters of the

Knights of the First Order. No. I fully intended to use my insider knowledge of Mack's movements to intercept him between his home and the office. Mack Quaid and I had always enjoyed a collegial relationship and I needed to take advantage of that now. Even if Maeron was smart enough to have eyes on both locations, I'd avoid detection by cornering Mack somewhere in between.

I positioned myself in an alley across the street from Mack's favorite bakery. Knowing Mack, he'd eat the porridge lovingly prepared by his wife and then stop for a pastry on his way to work. The man had a weakness for scones and I wasn't afraid to exploit it.

I turned invisible and left the safety of the alley. I made it as far as the corner when I felt a familiar twinge. The hairs on the back of my neck pricked and I was relieved no one could see me. Still, I held my breath as three butterflies soared past me. I didn't want to give the vampires a reason to hover. My stomach muscles clenched and I waited to release the breath until the butterflies were a safe distance from me. I had no way of knowing whether they'd been sent by Maeron or whether their appearance here was simply a coincidence. My money was on the former.

I waited on the corner with one eye trained on the bakery and the rest of me on high alert for more vampires. Just as I was about to abandon the plan, Mack's broad shoulders and round, cheerful face sauntered into view. Thank the gods.

I hurried across the street as the knight reached for the door handle. "Mack!"

He stopped and looked around.

"Mack, it's me. London."

He squinted at the empty air. "Why are you invisible?"

"Because I don't want anybody to see me. Why else?"

"So you'd rather me look crazy to passersby? I have a reputation to protect."

I arched an eyebrow. "Your mean your reputation that includes running across a cricket field holding a hydra head in each hand?"

"I was in the middle of a quest."

I clucked my tongue. "Somebody's defensive before he's had his carbs."

He glanced at the bakery window. "Why not come to the office?"

"Can't. Too risky."

He sighed. "What have you gotten yourself into this time?"

"You say that like I'm some kind of magnet for trouble."

"Why don't you think about that statement for two seconds? There's a reason we get along, you know."

"Fine." I materialized. "I'm a magnet for trouble. Will you help me?"

Chuckling, he shook his head. "If you weren't the best knight I've ever met, I'd stay as far away from you as possible."

"Gee, thanks."

"Hey, there's a compliment in there." He inclined his head toward the bakery. "Come with me. There's a back room." Without waiting for a response, he opened the door. "Ezra, my man, we need a little privacy."

The pastry chef behind the counter nodded as he slid a tray of croissants onto the shelf.

Mack crossed the room like he owned the place. "And bring a scone and a green tea, would you?"

He ducked into the narrow hallway and I followed. The shop was deeper than it looked. We turned right at the back of the building and he opened a door to an adjacent room.

I stopped short at the sight of a Ping-Pong table. There was also a billiard table. And a dartboard on the wall. And a pinball machine that featured dinosaurs and a comet.

My gaze swept the room. "What is this?"

Mack relaxed in the deep recliner. "A sanctuary of sorts."

Another sanctuary. Hopefully this visit didn't end in betrayal. "Why haven't you ever mentioned it before?"

He fixed me with a hard look. "Do I know all your secrets?"

I averted my gaze but said nothing.

"Thought as much." He pulled the handle to activate the footrest and exhaled. "That's the stuff."

"Why have I gone to the trouble of bribing you with scones when you've had special treatment all this time?"

Mack grinned. "Like I'm going to complain about more scones." He patted his stomach. "Although my wife occasionally does. Life's too short to say no."

"I can think of a few instances where that motto might get you into trouble."

He slotted his fingers and rested his hands behind his head. "I heard you were out of town."

"I was. Now I'm back."

"And what's with the cloak-and-dagger routine?"

"Someone is looking for me and I don't want to be found."

"Prince Maeron still hot on your heels?"

I blinked. "How'd you know?"

"Do you think I exist in a vacuum? Word gets around."

I shouldn't have been surprised. It wasn't every day agents of House Lewis stormed the Pavilion. "And do those words include the reason why he's looking for me?"

The door opened and Ezra entered carrying a tray. My stomach rumbled as I inhaled the aroma of the scones and was pleased to see he'd brought two plates and a pot of tea. Although I didn't especially like the taste of green tea, I wasn't about to complain.

Ezra set the tray on the side table next to the recliner. "Saw a butterfly patrol go by just now. Thought you'd want to know."

"Cheers, Ezra." Mack sat forward and snatched a scone from the plate. "Mhm. Cinnamon. My favorite."

"You seem to have a new favorite every week," Ezra said.

"Keeps you in business, doesn't it?"

"You're not kidding. Without your bottomless pit, I wouldn't be able to afford my rent." Laughing, Ezra left the room and closed the door behind him.

Mack motioned to the tray. "Help yourself, Hayes. You know you want to."

I didn't have to be told twice. I picked up a scone and devoured it in three large bites.

Mack shook his head as he poured the tea. "Those are some attractive table manners you've got."

"I haven't eaten much lately."

"Working too hard?"

"Imprisonment."

"Ah." He ate his scone slowly, savoring each bite. "How can I help?"

"I need somewhere to lay low while I figure things out."

"How exactly do you figure things out when the prince of House Lewis is hunting you? Is he suddenly going to lose interest?"

No. Not Maeron. And not while I had possession of the stones.

"I can't go back to the flat and I can't go to the Pavilion. And the menagerie needs me." It was too risky to tell Mack about the stones.

"I have it on good authority your animal friends are safe, Snow White."

"Glad to hear it, but I still don't want them to think I abandoned them." I pictured Big Red, the red panda, curled up on the sofa and watching the door with forlorn eyes for any sign of my return.

"Why not stay with one of the Boudica babes?"

I angled my head. "Seriously?"

He winced. "Sorry. I spent last night at the pub with the team. You know John rubs off on me."

John was a knight who worked for Mack. His misogynist streak prompted requests for things like a Knights of Boudica calendar that featured us wearing only our weapons. Only when Kami threatened to shove her crossbow into his largest cavity did he finally stop—at least in our presence.

"I can't stay with any of them," I said. "Maeron already had his men at the Pavilion. No doubt he has a list of their names and addresses." I sipped the tea. "Besides, the other knights don't know I'm back yet."

Mack slurped his tea and poured another cup. "Planning to tell them?"

"Yes, soon. I wanted to get situated first."

Mack waved a hand airily. "What about here?"

I frowned. "The secret recreation room in the bakery?"

He patted the side of the chair. "This is so comfortable it should be illegal."

"What about Ezra?"

"Ezra's on my payroll. He won't talk."

"Even if someone offers him more money?" And nobody had more money in the city than House Lewis.

"Have I ever let you down?"

"Several times. Want me to name them?"

Mack sighed. "If I tell you he won't talk, he won't talk."

I surveyed the room. It would have to do. "I do like to play darts." It was good target practice too.

"I'll tell Ezra to feed you. I know you're not the best at taking care of yourself."

I scoffed. "I take care of myself very well, thank you very much."

His gaze lingered on me. "I'm not talking about fighting, Hayes."

I didn't want to focus on my well-being, not when there were more important matters to discuss. "Since you're so knowledgeable about what happens in the city, have you heard about any strange occurrences this week?"

He wiped the crumbs from his lips. "Define strange. It was raining toads over in Chelsea two days ago. Got hired to investigate. Make sure it wasn't evidence of a new plague."

"Was it?"

"Nah. Just a couple young wizards working on a school project." Mack wagged a finger at me. "You've got to stop wearing your worry on your face, Hayes. The boys are fine. You know education is an exception."

Mack was referring to the law that prohibited magic except in certain circumstances. If you got caught and your actions didn't fall under one of the exceptions, the penalty was death. One method vampires used to maintain control was to suppress the power of the other species. Collectively witches and wizards had immense power, but they didn't function well as a unit. Instead they accepted comfortable jobs in agriculture and defense and allowed the vampires to govern unchecked. Werewolves were more adept at working together as a group, but their primary power was brute strength which wasn't enough to throw off the shackles of vampire rule.

"Anything else happen?"

Mack attempted to pour another cup of tea, but the pot was empty. "Oh, this one you'll find distressing. The library's closed for renovations."

"Closed?" The library never closed. One of its perks was that it was open twenty-fours a day, seven days a week. A perk I routinely took advantage of.

"Thought you'd be interested in that tidbit." Mack motioned to my half empty cup. "You going to finish that?"

I slid the cup toward him. "Green tea isn't my favorite."

"You might want to tell Ezra that or you'll end up with a pot of green tea outside the door each morning." Mack pointed to a door to the left of the dartboard. "Facilities are in there. Shower, sink, and toilet. Sorry, no bathtub to soak your sore muscles."

"I rarely have time to soak anyway." My tub at the flat was primarily for the animals.

"You should make time. It's one of the few luxuries I allow myself. Add some bubbles and it's pure decadence."

"We're surrounded by creature comforts and you're trying to tell me a bath is one of your few luxuries."

"Speaking of which…" Mack rose to his feet, knees cracking. "Want to play a game before I head out? Fair warning, though, I play a mean game of pinball."

Clever Mack, appealing to my competitive nature. I was tired, satiated, and—for the moment—safe. I could spare a few minutes.

My gaze landed on the pinball machine and I smiled. "Sure, why not? I never get tired of watching you lose."

4

The Britannia Library was one of the better-preserved buildings in the city. Prior to the Great Eruption, it was only open during business hours. Then ten supervolcanoes erupted, monsters emerged, the Eternal Night fell, and vampires decided to eschew the old-fashioned idea of operating according to the sun's schedule. There were still periods of awake and asleep, of course, but schedules in general were more flexible.

I walked up to the library door, already invisible. The library was close to my flat, which meant I had to stay out of sight as much as possible in case Maeron had his men posted in the area. I was also about to break into a closed building owned by House Lewis so invisibility was essential to the task.

The library boasted three Head Librarians and each one lived in the building itself. I was willing to bet that at least one of them was still on the premises. Fingers crossed it was Pedro. Pedro Gutierrez was the one librarian I could count on. He was the only human of the three librarians and the most tolerant of my unusual research requests.

I peered through the glass and tried to get a sense of what was happening inside the building. The official 'closed for renovations' announcement had to be a cover. I wondered whether another member of House Lewis made any inquiries regarding the renovations or whether they'd simply accepted what Maeron told them. It was possible they weren't even aware of the closure. It wasn't as though the royal vampires turned up in the Reading Room to reacquaint themselves with Shakespeare.

I pressed my face against the glass for a better view. There was no sign of movement in the darkness. No sign of construction either. It was time to make a move.

As I turned to round the building and find a less visible entry point, a silhouette in motion caught my eye. Pedro sauntered through the murk holding a paper bag and whistling to himself. Beethoven Symphony No. 5. Why did his choice of classical music not surprise me?

I watched and waited. The scent of onion and garlic lingered in the air as he passed by. He fished a key from his pocket and unlocked the door. I slipped in behind him before the door closed.

The interior was steeped in darkness. Pedro ambled along without needing a light. I followed directly in his footsteps to avoid tripping.

He arrived at a door marked 'Staff Only' and pushed it open with his shoulder. Switching on the light, he crossed the room and set the bag of food on the small counter. The room was set up like a studio flat. There was a single bed, a desk piled with books, a kitchenette, a small table and chair, and another door to what was presumably a bathroom. A large wardrobe and a chest of drawers took up half the far wall. I smiled when I spotted the stacks of books pushed underneath the bed. Pedro had an entire library at his disposal, yet still found it necessary to hoard books in his room.

I closed the door behind us with a soft click. "Pedro, don't panic."

He gasped and spun toward the sound of my voice. I turned myself visible and held up my hands to reassure him. "I'm not here to hurt you."

His shoulders relaxed at the sight of me. "I know that, Miss Hayes."

"Can you tell me why the library is closed?"

He smiled. "Are you that desperate for knowledge?"

"No." I hesitated. "Yes."

Pedro turned to the counter and began to empty the contents of the bag. "You don't believe it's under renovation?"

"I didn't see any tarps or butt cracks along the way, so no."

He opened a container and pulled a fork from the drawer. "Can I interest you in a plate of pasta? I have plenty."

My mouth opened to refuse but my stomach had other plans. I succumbed to the hunger pains. One scone does not a meal make.

"Are there meatballs? I'm a vegetarian."

"Only spaghetti. The sauce is magnificent. The cook is a refugee from mainland Europe and his skills are pure magic." Pedro gestured to the table. "Sit."

"There's only one chair. Where will you sit?"

"I've eaten on the bed more times than I care to count." He divided the spaghetti in half and scooped a section onto a plate, then handed me a fork. "Wine?"

I balked. "You have wine?"

I caught the hint of a smile. "There are perks to this job.

House Lewis gives me a dozen bottles of wine at Christmas and I open one bottle each month."

"I couldn't possibly accept."

"I insist." He opened a cupboard and pulled down a bottle and two stemmed glasses. "This is from a vineyard owned by House Russo."

An Italian red. I could smell the bouquet before the glass reached my nose. Divine.

"You'd think House Lewis would push their own wine."

"I drank theirs in January out of respect. Each bottle is from a different House."

I tasted the wine and nearly melted into a puddle on the floor. It was that good.

Pedro leaned against the counter and ate his spaghetti straight from the container. "Tell me, Miss Hayes, what research is so important that you've broken into a closed library?"

"First I'd like to know who closed the library."

"Prince Maeron."

Box one ticked. "Did he say why?"

"He has a team doing research and he doesn't want them disturbed."

My eyebrows lifted. "He has a team here now?"

"Lunch break. They're between shifts at the moment. I expect the afternoon shift to arrive shortly."

I wrapped the spaghetti around my fork. "What are they researching?"

"There's a list of topics. They seem to have divided the subjects between them. I'm to be on hand to assist and answer any questions."

"What about the other two librarians?" I let the sauce linger in my mouth. Pedro wasn't kidding. My tastebuds were in overdrive.

"They were sent on holiday."

"But not you?"

"I volunteered." He shrugged. "I have nowhere else to go." He twirled the spaghetti around his fork with expert precision and popped it into his mouth.

"Do you have a copy of the list of topics?"

Pedro peered at me over the top of his wine glass. "Why do I get the distinct impression you already know what they are?"

"I have a few guesses, but I'd like to be certain."

Pedro took a careful sip of wine. Then he set down the glass and approached his desk. "They seem mainly interested in summoning magic." He removed a sheet of paper from the desk and gave it to me. *Summoners* was written at the top.

Of course. The stones we'd discovered so far didn't include summoning magic. It made sense that the remaining stone would encompass that type of magic. Joseph Yardley's teleportation and my pocket dimension abilities would both fall under that magic umbrella.

I set the paper beside me and demolished the plate of pasta in under five minutes. "Are they also looking for news articles about unusual summoning activity?"

Pedro brightened. "As a matter of fact, yes. They even have a map where they've been pinpointing areas where summoning magic is more active."

I gulped down the rest of the wine. As delicious as it was, there was no time for sipping. "Can I see it?"

"It's in the Reading Room." His gaze darted to the door. "You should hurry. They'll be here any minute."

I looked at the list in an effort to memorize it.

"Take it with you," Pedro said. "I can always say I lost mine."

I folded the paper and stuck it in my pocket. "Thank you for this." I eyed the empty plate. "And the meal."

"You're welcome. Now hurry."

I exited his hovel and raced to the Reading Room. I located the light and switched it on. I spotted the map on one of the semi-circular counters and rushed forward to view it. There was a red X marked in three counties— Northumberland, Durham, and Cumbria. All three were located in the north, closer to the border with House Duncan.

Had Maeron already sent teams to these locations or had the researchers not yet reported their findings? From the open books and the papers scattered across the nearby surfaces, the information still seemed to be in the gathering phase.

I noticed a pile of newspapers and scanned the headlines.

Unexplained portal opens near site of old Durham Cathedral.

Monster infestation near Mitford.

Carlisle coven battles influx of ogres.

Young vampire in Temple Sowerby believed to have fallen down a flash portal, not a well as previously believed.

None of these places were particularly close to each other. They were, however, in each of the three counties identified. I wasn't persuaded by any of them that there was evidence of a stone with summoning power though. A monster infestation could mean anything. We had them in Britannia City all the time. Ogres could have been hired by Glendon to terrorize the northern borderlands.

I unfolded the paper to read the rest of the article. Maybe there was more information that made the vampires think these were viable leads.

A noise behind me interrupted my train of thought and I

turned to see a pigeon flying straight toward me. I had no doubt the bird was a warning from Pedro.

The vampires were on their way.

I folded the paper and placed it back on top of the pile. I managed to turn invisible just as two vampires waltzed into the room, deep in conversation. I crept to the far side of the room to avoid detection.

"That mushroom risotto is better than sex," I overhead the taller vampire say.

"If you really believe that, then you need a new partner," his companion replied.

"I won't tell him you said that."

"I'm bored of mushrooms. I feel like fungi is second only to blood in my house." The shorter vampire approached the map. "The prince wants an update tomorrow, but I don't think we'll be ready."

"We'll be ready with an update. We just might not be ready with as much information as he wants." The vampire spared a glance for the doorway. "The others should be here soon. If we can convince Dudley to stop messing around, we might make some headway."

"That'll only happen if the satellites go down again. He's glued to his phone."

I tiptoed out of the room. If more vampires were on the way, it was best to make myself scarce.

My heart thrummed as I hurried to the exit. Two more vampires entered and I pressed my back to the wall until they passed, grateful for my invisibility power.

"There's no way I can go to Cumbria," the vampire on the left said. "My son has a piano recital this weekend and my wife will kill me if I miss it."

"I don't think the prince will send us anyway," his companion said. "We usually get stuck doing the grunt work and he gives Bonnie's team the more glamorous assignments."

"I hardly think a trip to Cumbria is glamorous. Besides, it could be worse. We could be sent to Durham or Northumberland." He shuddered. "Don't fancy being near that wind that blows off the North Sea."

"I don't see the point of going until we can pinpoint an exact location. What are we meant to do—dig up entire towns? The stone could be hidden anywhere."

They continued talking but moved out of earshot.

I waited until they entered the Reading Room to bolt for the door.

Fresh air filled my lungs and I ran away from the building, only turning visible once I was certain the coast was clear. The visit to the library had been more fruitful than I expected. I'd confirmed my suspicions, glimpsed their progress, and left with a list of their research topics. More importantly, I'd enjoyed a plate of spaghetti with the most amazing sauce I'd ever tasted and a glass of wine.

I owed Pedro big time.

5

Going to the Pavilion to see the knights would be like wearing a red dress to a vampire ball. Instead I waited inside The Crown. My colleagues were creatures of habit, which meant they'd show up within the hour. At the moment, there were only two werewolves nursing their drinks across the room. Their faces were bruised and they looked like they were ready to drop. I sat at the counter and chatted with Simon, the werewolf that owned the pub.

"What's the deal with those two?" I whispered. "Shouldn't those bruises be healed already?"

Simon shook his head. "They're boxers. They've taken so many beatings, they've wrecked their systems. Every time they come in here, they seem to have suffered a bit more damage."

"Unlike this pub," I said. "I'm amazed how quickly the repairs happened."

The Crown had suffered significant damage when the Transcendence Stone paid a visit to the pub, courtesy of the teenaged vampire who'd brought it here from Devon. Members of the West End Werewolf Pack had gone berserk as a result of the stone's influence. The upside was that the pack offered to assist Simon with the costly repairs.

Simon smiled at the stained-glass window. Although it wasn't exactly the same as before, the quality was apparent. "I'm very fortunate."

"Fortunate would be not having your pub destroyed in the first place."

"Maybe so, but then I wouldn't have met Dallas."

I frowned. "Who's Dallas?"

"General contractor for the pack. Managed this job and quite effectively too." He straightened. "Your friends are here."

I swiveled on the stool.

Kami was the first to spot me. Her blond hair was knotted in a French braid and her skin looked a shade darker than usual. Looked like someone had been experimenting with a bronzing brush again.

"London?" She rushed forward with her arms spread wide. Instead of hugging me, though, she gave my arms a firm whack of displeasure.

"Ouch." I rubbed the injured areas. "What was that for?"

"What do you think?" Kamikaze Marwin was my best friend and clearly unafraid to tell me how she felt about my absence. "You left here under a cloud of secrecy. Made us tangle with a vampire prince and take care of the animals. Then nothing. No communication to say you're alive and well. Not a word until now."

"I'm sorry."

"I know. You had your reasons. You always have them."

Minka Tarlock pushed her way to the front. Minka had naturally bronzed skin—no cosmetics required. It was a gift from her Asian father, along with her wide-set brown eyes and dark hair. Her uptight attitude was one hundred percent Minka. "Why are you here? Why not come to the Pavilion?"

"It isn't safe."

"For you?" Minka asked.

"Not for any of us if I turn up."

Kami laughed. "That ship has sailed, sister. Prince Maeron has eyes all over Piccadilly Circus."

"Which is why I slipped in here while I was invisible." I lifted my pint glass in salute.

Simon seemed to sense the tension in the air. "Why don't you get settled at your usual table and I'll bring pitchers?"

"And food," Stevie said. "I'm famished." If you were in the market for a water witch, you couldn't go wrong with Stevie Torrin. In her dark blue suit of magical armor and combat boots, she was dressed for action. The tips of her dark hair had been dyed silver since the last time I saw her. The accent color complemented the silver undertones of her brown skin.

"I have a chicken and potato pie and an artichoke casserole," Simon announced.

"We'll take the lot," Stevie said.

"It's only the three of you?" I asked.

Minka counted the names on her fingers. "Neera and Ione are chasing down a runaway gryphon and Briar has a dentist appointment."

Kami looked at me. "Is that a problem?"

"No."

It was good to see everyone again. So much had happened since we last saw each other. If I had any intention of telling them about the events in Scotland, I wouldn't know where to start.

Good thing I was keeping my mouth shut.

"How's the menagerie?" I asked.

"Missing you," Kami said. "Big Red's been depressed. He's barely eaten."

"Don't let him fool you. It's only a ruse to get treats." As much as I wanted to see them, I knew it wasn't smart. Our reunion would have to wait.

"We've taken turns with them," Stevie added. "Tried to keep two together, except for Hera, of course."

"That cat would perfectly happy on her own island," Kami said.

"No, she wouldn't," I replied. "Then who would she have to boss around?"

"Where are you staying?" Kami asked. "I take it you haven't gone back to your flat."

I shook my head. "I can't. And I'd rather not tell you where my base is."

Kami rolled her eyes. "The less we know, the better. Blah blah. Same old London."

Except I wasn't the same old London. Not really.

I debated whether to tell the other knights the secret of my parentage.

No.

The same threats existed as before. It wouldn't be fair to burden them with knowledge they didn't request. Telling them would be for my sake not theirs and I wasn't that selfish.

"Are you officially back to work?" Minka asked.

I drank the ale and savored the familiar taste. It wasn't particularly good, but it tasted like home. Right now that was all I wanted.

"Not officially. There are a few things I need to do first."

"What could be more important than the Knights of Boudica?"

Kami snorted. "Only Minka would ask that question."

Stevie craned her neck. "Where's the pie?"

Kami placed a hand on her arm. "Easy, tiger. Simon is only one man."

"Then he should hire help. I'm starving."

"Tell me what I've missed," I said. It would distract Stevie from her hunger, and it had the added bonus of telling me whether there'd been any unusual activity related to the stones.

Minka clasped her hands on the table in schoolmarm fashion. "There was a missing wizard. That was an interesting case."

Stevie snorted. "He'd teleported into a tiger cage at the zoo and couldn't get out. He hid for three days until one of the keepers noticed him."

"Why didn't he flag down a keeper?" I asked.

"Fear paralysis," Minka said. "He said he was terrified if he made a peep that the tiger would attack him."

"Why did he teleport into the cage in the first place?" My mind immediately went to the final stone.

"He focused on the wrong street address," Stevie replied. "He was meant to teleport to a client's. He's a healer with special dispensation to perform magic."

Kami gulped a mouthful of ale. "I'm not sure I'd want someone healing me who couldn't remember my address."

The incident sounded like an innocent mistake rather than the influence of an ancient stone.

"How did you end up working on the case?" I asked.

"His wife called us," Minka said. "Sheila's my hairstylist."

"She bartered," Kami interrupted. "Can you imagine what would have happened if one of us had bartered for services? Hypocrisy thy name is Minka Tarlock."

Minka sniffed. "I've let the rest of you get away with far worse."

"Go easy on Minka," I said. "Technically, bartering has always been an option for our clients. We just don't emphasize it."

Simon delivered the pie and the casserole, along with a pile of plates. The sharp aroma of spices penetrated my nostrils.

"About time," Stevie said. "I was ready to eat Kami's arm."

Kami's eyebrows knitted together. "What's wrong with your own arm?"

Stevie held it up for inspection. "Not enough meat on these bones."

Kami held her arm next to Stevie's for comparison. "Fair enough."

Once everyone was full of food and ale, I made my pitch.

"I could use your help soon."

Kami stopped mid-chew. "Soon? What does that mean? Are we waiting for a celestial event?"

Stevie groaned. "It's not another sacrifice, is it? I've barely recovered from the last one."

"It isn't a celestial event. I just don't know the timing yet. I'd like more intel first."

"At least you're giving us advanced notice, although it would be best if I can schedule it." Minka swept her fork through the casserole. "Paid commitments will have to take priority."

Kami met my gaze and silently shook her head. I knew I could count on her.

"I'd also like to brainstorm ideas for a different task. This one I intend to do on my own." The casserole was incredible. The melody of flavors Simon had blended together created a perfect culinary symphony.

Minka scrunched her nose. "What kind of task? Why do I get the feeling this is dangerous?"

"Because it's London. Of course it's dangerous." Kami pinned me with an enthusiastic look. "What is it?"

"Let's say hypothetically that someone wanted to break into the Tower and steal an object..."

Minka started to choke. Stevie whacked her on the back until Minka pushed her to stop.

"Do you mean the Tower that stores the House jewels?" Stevie asked.

"And prisoners awaiting execution?" Kami added.

Minka reached for her glass and drank. "Can you at least lower your voice when you discuss treason?" she asked in a hoarse whisper.

"I have a few ideas," Kami said.

"Me too," Stevie added.

Minka glared at them. "No helping. Not with this." She turned her judgmental gaze to me. "What can you possibly want to take from there? It isn't like you need jewels."

"Nobody *needs* jewels," Kami said, "but they sure can liven up an ensemble."

Minka's fingers curled tightly around her fork. "Need I remind you that we are knights? We are not having this conversation."

Later, Kami mouthed.

Stevie's phone vibrated on the table and she scanned the message. "Oh, boy." She sank a lot of feelings into that simple expression.

Kami shot her a quizzical look. "What's up?"

"There are sepa demons on Waterloo Bridge. Mr. Richards is requesting a team."

Lyle Richards owned a corner shop not far from the bridge. He hired us every quarter to sweep the alley behind the shop and eliminate any potential threats. We were basically his supernatural exterminators. The bridge, however, was a much bigger deal.

"How many?" I asked.

Minka frowned. "Knights?"

"Demons."

Stevie scraped back her chair and stood. "He says they're covering an entire section of the bridge and seem to be crawling out of the woodwork."

"The bridge is made of metal," Minka pointed out.

Stevie sighed. "It's just an expression."

"Why call you?" Simon asked as he cleared the empty plates. "Won't House Lewis send help?"

"Not as quickly as we'll get there," Stevie said. "You know how vampire bureaucracy works. They don't care about Lyle's business."

Sepa demons were like centipedes the size of alligators that multiplied if you didn't get them under control. We'd eliminated a few a month ago lurking near Embankment, but it was possible we missed one or two—and a couple was two too many.

"We should stop by the armory," Stevie suggested. "I don't have any weapons with me."

Kami clapped me on the shoulder. "We have London. We don't need the armory."

I glared at her. "No pressure."

Kami lit up. "You're really coming? I assumed you'd say no."

"I said I wasn't officially back in the office, but I can certainly help with sepa demons, but you *will* need weapons." It wasn't as though Maeron would be watching every nook and cranny in the city. Sepa demons were no joke. If the banner needed me, I was on board.

"With all of us working together, we should be able to dispatch them quickly," Stevie said.

"If London is going, then I'll stay," Minka said. "It's not like I'm very useful in the field anyway."

I opened my mouth to object but Kami nudged me.

"You can pay the bill," Kami said to Minka.

"Good to see you again, London," Simon said. "I try not to worry about my patrons. Some make it easier than others."

I smiled. He sounded like Mack.

I was relieved when Kami and Stevie swung by the armory for weapons while I waited for them in an alley near The Crown. I didn't want to resort to any magic that might draw a royal eye to the bridge.

Kami appeared at the entrance to the alley loaded down with enough weapons to intimidate a small army.

I adopted my most official-sounding voice. "Excuse me, miss, but do you have the appropriate permits for that crossbow and the..." My voice faltered. "You brought a flamethrower?"

"You can control fire," Kami said. "We'll burn these suckers to ash. Teamwork makes the dream work, remember?"

I looked at Stevie who simply shrugged.

Together we headed to the bridge. It was close enough from the Circus to travel on foot, which was preferable given the number of weapons we carried. I'd been known to ride the bus with an axe strapped to my back, but a crossbow and flamethrower would probably get us barred by the driver. Emphasis on probably. It really depended on the driver.

"Why didn't you let me argue with Minka?" I asked.

"Because she's not going to change," Kami said. "She's comfortable and unless something dramatic happens to make her painfully uncomfortable, she's going to stick to her shell."

I thought of my own situation. Was it the same for me? Would I stick to my lies and deception unless and until my situation became too painfully uncomfortable to tolerate?

Maybe.

Of course my situation was different. Minka wouldn't die by forcing herself outside of her comfort zone whereas I would almost certainly sign my death warrant.

Hmm. On second thought, Minka could die too.

"Tell me what happened to you," Kami urged. "I want to know you're okay."

"I'm here, aren't I? I'm clearly okay."

She gave me a pointed look. "I know you, London."

"I'm not ready to get into detail."

"Then get into big concepts. I don't need the leaves on the trees, but at least give me a freakin' forest."

I shook my head. I didn't want to talk about Callan or House Duncan.

"Did you at least get the stones you were looking for?"

I held up my index finger.

"Better than nil," Kami said. She slapped an arm along my shoulders. "We really missed you."

"Totally," Stevie agreed. "Trio missed you the most, I think. She kept going over to your desk and whining."

I narrowed my eyes at them. "Are you saying all this because you thought I was dead?"

Kami groaned. "Good grief. Learn to accept a compliment."

"Compliment accepted." I unsheathed my axe and loosened my shoulders. "Let's get rid of these demons before we have to rebuild a bridge."

We arrived at the bridge and I immediately wanted to change my mind.

"Holy hellfire," Stevie breathed.

Kami swallowed hard. "You can say that again."

Each demon had to have at least one hundred legs. Their segmented bodies made them look like caterpillars that had endured a nuclear blast.

"Their legs are like yours, London," Kami said.

"Covered in fine hair?"

"No, freakishly long."

"When I had centipedes in my flat, I stomped on them," Stevie said.

Kami contemplated the scurrying sepa demons. "Call me crazy, but I don't think stomping is going to work with these guys."

One advantage to their large size was that they couldn't hide easily. The only crevices big enough to hide them were actual craters. Unlike their insect counterpart, however, their forciples were powerful enough to penetrate our skin. Thank the gods for magical armor.

"Sticky traps?" Kami suggested.

Stevie wrinkled her nose. "And watch them leave half their legs behind and keep running? No thanks."

"Maybe we should try to trap them from both sides of the bridge," Kami said. "Keep them contained."

South of the Thames was vampire central. It wasn't a part of the city any of us wanted to venture if we could help it, especially me.

"Let's see what we can accomplish from this side first," I told them.

We waded into the sepa stew. They moved fast for their

size and shape. Must be the multitude of legs. No matter what we threw at them, though, they seemed to keep coming.

"Don't forget they thrive in moisture," I yelled.

"Why do you think I brought this?" Kami opened the ignition valve on the flamethrower and pressed the button. "Do you forget where we live? Might as well change the name to Moist City." Fire streamed from the nozzle and flooded the scampering demons.

Stevie gave her a dark look. "You did not just use that word."

"Sorry, Damp City," Kami called with a meek smile.

I sliced through the middle of a demon and watched as its two halves ran away from each other before collapsing. "I'm just trying to brainstorm."

"What's your suggestion then? Drain the river?" The stream of fire ceased and Kami frowned at the empty nozzle. "A little help with fire magic, please?"

I lowered Babe and concentrated on the flames still raging across the bridge. I grabbed control of the area closest to me and created a fiery wall to prevent their escape. I was on the wrong side of the wall with my back to the south end of the bridge, but I could run through the flames if necessary.

Kami appeared behind me with the flamethrower.

"What are you waiting for?" I urged. "Shoot these guys."

"First I want you to agree to let me help you."

I jerked my hand toward the encroaching demons. "I'm agreeing. Do it!"

"I'm not talking about these guys. I'm talking about your plan for the Tower."

I gaped at her. "Are you serious right now?"

A group of demons surged toward us, their little legs moving at a rapid pace. "Okay, I agree. Do it!"

She covered them with a fiery blanket.

Nevertheless the demons persisted.

Kami regarded them with a mixture of frustration and respect. "These sepa demons are surprisingly resistant to fire."

"So much for your theory," I said.

Like some species, they'd apparently managed to build up a tolerance over time. At least the fire would draw out a portion of the moisture and weaken them.

Draw out the moisture.

I could do that. It wouldn't be easy with so many of the demons still kicking, but the dagger was in, so to speak, and they were quickly losing strength. I only needed to twist the blade.

I doused the flames and released my connection to them before shifting to water magic. There might be questions later about my ability to seamlessly switch between elements. I took great pains to hide the extent of my powers. With everyone preoccupied at the moment, it was a minor risk and one I was willing to take.

I focused on the water molecules and secured my connection. It wasn't easy to block the connection to the river. The Thames demanded attention.

I ignored the call of the river and kept my focus on the water molecules in front of me. Closing my eyes, I pulled them toward me like ingots of iron to a magnet. I'd be soaking wet by the time I finished thanks to this sepa demon shower. I'd need a proper shower afterward, preferably one that involved a scrub brush and bleach.

I heard a massive crunching sound and opened my eyes

in time to see Stevie smashing a demon into pieces and kicking its dried-out carcass into the river.

"Now that's a satisfying sound," Kami remarked, giving the same treatment to the demon by her feet. "Almost as good as bubble wrap."

Starved of moisture, the demons were reduced to empty shells. The knights proceeded to sweep them off the bridge and watched the current drag them away.

"The sea monsters will appreciate the free snacks," Stevie said.

Kami peered at the water below. "Circle of life, my friend. We're all food for the fishes."

"I thought it was worms," Stevie said.

"I'm not food for anyone if I can help it," I said. "Torch me when I die, remember?"

"I believe that's a provision in all our contracts," Stevie said.

It was one thing to be food for worms, but nobody wanted to end up as food for vampires.

Kami jogged over to me wearing a broad smile. "See? Teamwork makes the dream work."

"If this is your idea of a dream, I'd hate to see your nightmares," Stevie remarked.

I glanced at the Tower which was visible from the bridge. I was about to walk into a nightmare of my own creation and, even worse, I was bringing my best friend with me.

6

Gathering my weapons, I cursed myself for honoring my bargain with Kami. I hoped she'd forget the agreement by the time we left the bridge, but I should've known better. Once Kami got a bee in her bonnet, there was no stopping her. I shared my current address and we made a plan to meet in the morning.

The next day she arrived at the secret room in the bakery wearing a hot pink wig and a cloak that looked three times too big for her. She also held a half-eaten muffin in her hand.

I gave her a curious look from the recliner. "Dare I ask?"

"I'm in disguise. Maeron's guys are watching for a hot blonde with a butt like two steel orbs. If they see me now, they'll only see pink hair and an oversized body."

"You do have a good butt," I acknowledged.

Kami surveyed the recreation room. "Mack is a genius." She crossed the room and thrust the muffin half at me. "It's chocolate chip."

"No thanks. I've eaten." Ezra had insisted on serving me

a cheese and apple pastry so delicious it would've made Mack weep.

She angled her head toward the Ping-Pong table. "I don't suppose you fancy a match before we go?"

"I don't know. Do we need to stop by the armory?"

Kami unbuttoned her cloak and threw it back to reveal a plethora of weapons strapped to her body.

"Kami, you can't wear all that to the Tower. You'll get yourself killed."

"I don't intend to use them unless absolutely necessary."

"The whole point is for me to sneak in and out unnoticed. Any use of weapons will get us noticed."

"Get *me* noticed."

"Kami, I am not letting you get hauled away by House Lewis guards."

"I have no intention of being hauled away. I'm a knight, too, remember? Just because you're the powerhouse of our duo doesn't mean I'm any less capable."

She had a point.

"What's the plan?"

"I'll keep them distracted," Kami said. "You run in."

My mind jerked back to Cynthia as she jumped from the dragon.

"No."

Kami cocked her head. "What's up? I distract. You sneak. We've done this bit more times than I can count."

"This is different."

"If you're so concerned, why not ask Callan to get you in?"

I bristled and she lunged. I shouldn't have bristled.

"I knew it! What happened?"

"We had a disagreement. It was my fault. That's all I'm

going to say." I didn't tell her about Cynthia. The wound was too fresh.

"More secrets," Kami huffed. "Shocker."

I shot her a warning glare. "Whatever happens, do not come in after me and don't hang around. Once I'm inside, you're out of there. I mean it, Kami. Don't try to be a hero or I will never forgive you."

No more blood on my hands, please and thank you very much.

Kami held up a hand. "I solemnly swear to not be a hero, even though technically I'm a knight and it's supposed to be part of the package."

"Knights were never truly heroes. My mother..."

Kami tipped back her head. "We don't have time for another Rhea Hayes history lesson. If you want to commit a high crime, we'd better boogie."

We left the bakery and Kami blew a kiss to Ezra on the way out.

"New best friend?" I asked.

"The man makes pastries, London. If he isn't careful, I might marry him."

I laughed. For a fleeting moment the events of recent weeks were forgotten. We were simply London and Kami, flirting with a fabulous baker boy and preparing for magic mischief.

We rode the bus to the Tower and Kami ended up sandwiched between the broad shoulders of two businessmen. She didn't seem to mind.

The dark-haired man to her right looked her up and down. "Cosplay?"

Kami glowered at him. "Have you never seen a knight before?"

He broke into an amused smile. "Right. And if I rip open

this white collared shirt, you'll see my red 'S'." He leaned closer. "That's Superman's outfit."

Kami's glowering intensified.

I leaned back and smiled at the would-be superhero. "You might want to watch your step. She can control minds."

He chuckled.

"It's not a power I take lightly," Kami interjected. "I try to use it sparingly and rely on my other talents instead."

"And what are those? Knitting and baking?" He scrutinized her. "Definitely baking. Looks like someone enjoys her sugar and carbs."

"No, don't!"

Too late. The man didn't know what hit him. Well, he knew because it was his own fist.

"Let him go," I said. "He's not worth it."

"And he thinks I'm not worth it."

"See? You're in agreement."

The man to the left of Kami vacated his seat and moved to the back of the bus.

Blood trickled from the businessman's nose. The bus pulled aside for the next stop and we hurried off. Kami waited until she reached the pavement to release her hold on him.

"Sorry," she said. "He deserved it."

"Are you trying to get yourself killed over a jackass like that? You're the one who scolded me for using magic to ease a wizard's suffering and you're throwing magic around like a teenager."

Kami clenched her jaw. "I said I was sorry. He won't report the incident. He'll be too embarrassed to have been beaten by a woman."

"Technically he was beaten by a man."

She shoved her hands in her pockets. "What's the plan for the Tower?"

I cast a furtive glance around us. "I'm going to steal the Immortality Stone."

Kami choked back laughter. "The stone you said has been in House Lewis hands for centuries? The stone that holds the power of immortality?"

"I'm glad you remember all that. Saves me the trouble of reminding you."

It was foolish and risky, but I had to try. King Glendon wanted the Immortality Stone come hell or high water. He'd lost a war trying to get it. Then Callan had refused to steal it for him. I had no doubt he had men planted here to take it.

I had to get there first.

I'd been to the Tower once with Callan. He'd shown me the Immortality Stone as part of my investigation to find Davina and the Elemental Stone. It was clear at the time the two stones were related although no one knew how or why. As much as I would've liked to see him again, I couldn't ask him for a favor now, especially when he wanted nothing to do with me. Hell, there was a chance he'd turn me over to the authorities, although deep down I didn't think he would. I'd been fortunate enough to glimpse his gentler side during our travels. No matter how he felt about the secrets I'd revealed, he wasn't the Beast of Birmingham anymore.

I sensed a familiar presence and looked skyward and smiled. "Hey, you."

Barnaby swooped toward us and I held out my arm as a perch. The raven cawed.

"It's good to see you, too, friend. I'm sorry I was gone so long."

Barnaby ruffled his feathers.

"Don't worry," I reassured him. "I have a plan and Kami's here to help."

She bonked the raven's beak. "Everything's under control, B."

Barnaby's beady eyes met mine and I could see the concern reflected there.

"If you're that worried, feel free to lurk," I told him. "Just don't follow me inside. I don't want you within reach of any vampires. Some of them aren't particular about which blood they drink."

The raven cawed again and flew away.

Kami stripped off her weapons and hid them inside a collapsed stone wall. Between the two of us, we'd accumulated about three dozen hiding spots to stash personal belongings around the city.

"Ready?" Kami asked.

"You're not." I nodded to her uniform.

She glanced down. "Oh, right." She unzipped far enough to show off a little cleavage. Then she pulled her hair into a messy bun to expose her neck. "One of these fine attributes should draw their attention."

"It's a shame you can't walk in backward." I smacked her backside and turned invisible.

Together we approached the main gate. Kami stumbled and giggled, just a tipsy girl leaving an after-work gathering at the pub. She waved exuberantly at the guards.

"Hey, could someone help me? I seem to have lost my favorite piece of jewelry. Could one of you handsome blokes give me a pearl necklace?" She tossed back her head and laughed, giving them a prime view of her neck. "Oh my goodness, no. I mean help me find it." She hiccupped and covered her mouth.

Both guards on duty smiled at her like they'd never

spoken to an attractive woman before. Her work here was done. I slipped through the gate and made a beeline for the White Tower, the building that held the stone.

I hurried up the uneven stone steps and rushed along the corridor. An unseen hand blocked my path and sent me sliding backward across the floor.

What the hell?

I climbed to my feet and peered at the shadows. Two pale, wrinkled hands maneuvered gracefully against the inky backdrop of the corridor. I'd only seen hand movements like those once before.

"Cynthia?"

A dark hood dropped to a set of cloaked shoulders and revealed a smooth face. "London?"

I held my breath as my brain tried to comprehend. Cynthia was alive.

"How? Why?"

"I've been trying to find you. I'm glad to see you're safe."

"You tracked me here of all places?" I surveyed the stone walls. "How did you even get past the guards?"

"Same way I got past the guards at the border. I told you I'd distract them."

"I'd love to hear the details, but I'm sort of on a schedule right now." I gazed at her in wonder. "I thought you died."

"I almost did."

"You should go. I'm about to do something a tad naughty and you don't want to get caught with me."

"I'm afraid I can't let you do that." Cynthia extended a hand and blasted me with a wave of magic. I shot to the side and slammed against the wall.

I cracked my neck. "If you keep this up, you'll wake the neighbors."

"I'd rather not hurt you. I'm only here for the stone."

"What took you so long?"

"I had to make my way to the city. I only have two feet."

I flexed my fingers at my sides. "Why do you want the stone? You're not a vampire. The stone won't do anything for you."

"No, but turning it over to my king will."

Aha. I should've known. If I hadn't left the anti-magic chains on the Spirit Stone, maybe I would have.

"Do you even know what the stone does? Or did he leave that part out?"

Cynthia drew herself to her full height. "It's the reason House Lewis is so feared and powerful. Take the stone away and they'll crumble like a soft biscuit."

I couldn't help but smile. "Do you believe everything you're told?"

Her smile matched mine. "You're one to talk."

She was right. I'd believed her asylum story. Well played, Cynthia.

"I'm sorry, Cynthia. I can't let you give Glendon that stone. There's too much at stake."

"Then why are you here? It seems you have a selfish reason of your own."

I shook my head. "It's not for me. The stones unlock our potential. If the potential connected to that stone doesn't already exist in you, then the stone doesn't have any effect." No reason to get into the whole dhampir thing.

Cynthia's hands started their mesmerizing movements again. This time I didn't wait. I connected to my magic and gave the air a hard shove. Cynthia fell backward and I jumped over her body to continue down the corridor.

I halted in front of the display. For a split second I thought I'd arrived at the wrong section. There was a pedestal but no stone.

I looked left and right. This was definitely the right place.

"It's gone," I said.

Cynthia caught up to me and stretched her hands to blast me again.

I gave her a sideways glance. "Stop, Cynthia. The stone isn't here. See for yourself." I pointed to the empty pedestal.

Footsteps thundered toward us. Shit. Cynthia cost me precious time. Kami's performance was only enough to get me through the main gate. It wasn't enough to garner the attention of every guard on the inside.

Six guards flanked us.

"No, wait. You don't understand," Cynthia said.

"We understand you're trespassing," one of the guards said. "And you're to be taken into custody."

"No, no. There's been a misunderstanding. Talk to Prince Maeron. He'll vouch for me."

Prince Maeron and Glendon. It figured. That explained how Glendon knew about the stones.

"Prince Maeron is the one who gave us the order," the guard said.

Painful recognition streaked across Cynthia's features. She'd been double-crossed and she knew it.

"That bastard." She spat on the floor. "Well, I won't go willingly." She raised her hands.

"Cynthia, don't!"

The guard closest to her withdrew a gun and shot her in the chest. Blood seeped from the cloak. Her body slumped to the floor.

I stared at the fallen witch. There wouldn't be a second resurrection.

"Come on," a guard barked, pushing me.

The guards marched me down the uneven steps and

across the courtyard. Energy pulsed in the air and I instinctively looked up to see Barnaby. My eyes widened when I saw the flock of ravens behind him. It seemed that someone had gone in search of reinforcements. The birds were so numerous that they spread across the sky like a pot of spilled ink.

The ravens were finally returning to the Tower.

The vampires on the ramparts were the first to spot them.

"Incoming!" one shouted.

The birds began to dive-bomb the guards. Their arrival was so fast and unexpected that the vampires were quickly overwhelmed. The guards surrounding me seemed momentarily stunned and I seized the opportunity to escape.

"Where are the wizards?" another vampire yelled.

The ravens attacked from all sides. Barnaby swooped in front of me.

I ran.

I didn't make it to the gate. Green light exploded ahead, narrowly missing me. When I refocused, a line of wizards blocked my exit.

Terrific.

"Go," I told Barnaby.

Magic sparked from the wizards' hands and I flexed my fingers, debating how much force to use, when I felt the sting of metal. Chains wrapped around my wrists. I recognized the sensation of anti-magic chains.

Again.

I struggled against them anyway because I'm stubborn like that.

The wizards parted and a svelte figure strode toward me. His dark hair was neatly combed and his dark eyes were unamused.

My half-brother. Maeron.

His gaze met mine. "You know where to take her."

Four guards surrounded me and directed me toward another tower. I considered a headbutt and a few strategic kicks, but I highly doubted I'd make it through the wall of wizards without access to my magic.

I conserved my energy and went along without a fight. I didn't want to end up like Cynthia.

The guards pushed me through an open doorway and used their bodies to block the exit.

"You work as a door now?"

They moved aside and Maeron crossed the threshold.

"Leave us," he announced.

The guards scampered away like cockroaches in the light and the heavy door slammed shut behind us.

Maeron and I stood facing each other. It was difficult to look him in the eye, knowing everything I did.

"This place was once called the Tower of London." His lips curved into a malevolent smile. "Fitting, isn't it?"

I leaned my shoulder against the wall in an effort to maintain a casual air. I refused to let Maeron see me sweat. "I'm surprised your mother didn't name it after herself." It was the closest I dared get to a 'your mama' joke.

He glared at me. "What are you doing here? I would've expected you to remain in hiding instead of presenting yourself to me on a platter."

"Where's the Immortality Stone?"

He laughed. "You're hardly in a position to make demands, Miss Hayes."

"Let me make sure I have the story straight. You teamed up with Glendon, which is how Cynthia got across the border and lived to tell the tale. But then he tried to stab you in the back by sending Cynthia to steal the stone for him, only you stole it first." I feigned a thoughtful look. "How will you explain Cynthia's death to your cohort? She was his most trusted witch."

"Let me worry about that. You have more pressing concerns."

I ignored his threat. "Where's Callan?"

Maeron grunted. "I was wondering when you'd come around to the topic of my brother. He doesn't know you're here, nor will he."

"What's your plan? Kill me and toss me straight into the Thames?"

He pursed his lips and shrugged. "Not too far of a drop."

"And what happens when my body washes up?"

"You're a knight, Miss Hayes. Your occupation is inherently dangerous."

He had me there, except I still had a pretty persuasive bargaining chip. Three, in fact.

"If you kill me, you'll never find the stones."

"I assume that includes the real Elemental Stone."

I was wondering when he would figure out that I'd given his family a fake. "Took you long enough."

"I waited until my parents had moved on to other interests before I went to retrieve it. Imagine my surprise when my wizard said it was nothing more than a regular rock that someone had marked." He looked down his nose at me. "I assume that someone was you."

"Imagine my surprise when you said you have your own wizard."

His smile was unnervingly predatory. "Rest assured I don't intend to kill you straight away." He patted his jacket pocket. "I brought along a vial of truth serum. After all, it worked wonders for Romeo Rice."

And I knew what fate awaited the werewolf once he'd revealed what he knew about the Transcendence Stone.

I held out my bound wrists. "You'll have to release me from the anti-magic chains or the truth serum won't work."

Hesitation flickered in the vampire prince's eyes. He understood the risk. Good. Now it was his turn to sweat.

"Maeron?" The voice startled us both. Even more startling was the face of King Casek as he peered through the bars of the door. It was the first time I'd seen him since discovering the truth of my parentage. We were in the midst of a family reunion and I was the only one who knew it.

"Your Majesty," I said.

His gray eyes squinted. "Miss Hayes, is that you? What on earth are you doing in here?"

Maeron turned with a ready frown. "Terrible, isn't it? I received word that she'd been taken prisoner and I've come to see what the fuss was about."

The king opened the door and entered the cramped quarters. "I was told there was a disturbance in the Tower. That's why I came." His brow creased. "Was it something to do with you, Miss Hayes?"

"I'm afraid it's rather disturbing news," Maeron interjected. "A witch managed to bypass security. Miss Hayes is the one who caught her."

It seemed Maeron was now forced to alter his plan.

"How fortunate for us," the king said. "You seem to be our lucky penny."

I swallowed the lump in my throat. "I was passing outside the gates and heard a commotion. I offered to help. The guards recognized me and let me pass."

Maeron's eyes briefly met mine. "Unfortunately the witch managed to take something precious from us before she was killed."

And suddenly Maeron's plan became clear. Use Cynthia as a scapegoat for his own actions.

The king's gaze flicked from Maeron to me. "What did she take? Jewels?"

"The Immortality Stone," Maeron replied.

The king appeared unperturbed. "Well, she's dead now. Simply take it back from her."

Maeron inhaled deeply. "Not possible. She must've had summoning abilities. The stone was nowhere to be found."

I could've called his bluff right there and then, but the odds of King Casek believing me over Maeron were slim to none.

The king regarded Maeron. "What happened to our second line of defense? Surely the wizards could have dealt with one witch?"

"There will be a full inquiry."

The king seemed baffled. "How did she learn of the stone and why steal it? Was she working on behalf of someone else?"

"I was hoping to ask her those very questions, but alas." Maeron's broad shoulders sagged.

"I want a full report from security as soon as it's ready." The king pivoted to face me. "In the meantime, I'm more than happy to escort Miss Hayes to freedom."

Maeron bowed his head. "Yes, of course, Father." He shot me a parting glance before exiting the cell. It promised we'd meet again.

I didn't doubt it.

The king called for a guard to relieve me of my chains. The vampire was one of the guards who escorted me to the cell and he seemed understandably surprised by the reversal.

I rubbed my wrists. "Thank you, Your Majesty."

He issued orders to the guard as he left and turned back to me. I stared at the vampire king and a multitude of unasked questions burned my tongue. *Did you search for my mother? Did you conspire to murder Queen Britannia? How did you raise a son like Maeron?* I wish I could've asked the candle at the Atheneum these questions, but I'd been in shock. I couldn't blame myself for abandoning my original question.

Nope. Not asking. Don't have a death wish.

The king noticed my stare. "Is there something on your mind?"

I jerked to attention. "No, Your Majesty."

His eyes narrowed. "You lie."

"You don't want me to ask my question."

He chuckled. "Now you sound like Davina." He waved a hand airily. "I still owe you a debt, after all. You may ask with impunity. Fire away."

You may ask with impunity.

We both might live to regret that offer.

"If you insist." I cleared the fear from my throat. "The queen..."

"You have a question regarding Imogen?"

"Britannia."

Light flickered in his eyes. "Ah, I see. Go on then."

"There's evidence to suggest that her death was...avoidable."

He laughed. "Not going to war with House Duncan would've been a good start."

"Apologies, I chose the wrong word. I mean suspicious."

He cocked a royal eyebrow. "Suspicious?"

Was I really going to do this? Regardless of the answer, what did I hope to gain?

The truth. I wanted to know whether my father was the

kind of man who would murder his wife. Was he more like Glendon than I cared to admit?

"There've been rumors to suggest her death was the result of a deal...between Houses."

His expression remained shockingly neutral. It was a face Callan had also perfected.

"You're asking the king of House Lewis whether I conspired with the king of House Duncan to kill my wife during the battle to defend this city from Glendon's attack?"

I blanched. "Yes, Your Majesty."

He stiffened. "I won't dignify the question with a response."

My stomach plummeted. I felt a combination of guilt and relief. "Apologies..."

He cut me off. "What I am willing to confess is that I felt relief upon hearing the news."

I blinked at him. "Relief?"

"The queen was a walking, talking menace, not to mention a raging narcissist." He paused and observed me. "I can see you're shocked. A husband isn't meant to say such things about his own wife."

How did one respond to a king's admission? "I don't presume to know..."

"She always craved more, you see. There wasn't a line she was unwilling to cross. She would've carved a bloody path all the way to China if she'd lived. So, yes, I felt relieved that she was gone. The public mourned, while I quietly expressed gratitude for my good fortune."

I exhaled once I realized I'd stopped breathing. "I appreciate your candor, Your Majesty."

"I didn't love her. That would've made her death much more difficult, of course. Is that terrible to admit? Perhaps." He gazed past me. "I don't love Imogen either, but thankfully she lacks Britannia's insatiable need for glory and power and I needed to secure an alliance with a major House." He shrugged. "Osmond made the most sense at the time."

"Have you ever loved anyone?" The question slipped out before I could stop myself. My inner child was desperate to know.

His expression grew wistful. "Only once, but she wasn't of royal blood." He released a regretful chuckle. "She wasn't even of vampire blood. The relationship was doomed from the start."

My gut twisted. "Is that why you married Britannia instead? Because she ticked the right boxes?"

"Britannia and I were already married at the time. I suspect the queen knew about my dalliance, but we had a silent agreement not to discuss any diversions."

"It seems strange that someone with the queen's reputation was willing to overlook her competition."

He laughed. "Britannia would never have viewed her as competition or a threat. Her ego refused to allow it. She was remarkably jealous though. I would've ended the relationship to protect the woman's life if it had come to that. Britannia would've been keen to open her veins." He paused. "All of them."

"What do you mean 'if it had come to that?'"

He sighed. "There was no need. The woman ended the relationship first."

I remembered the vision of the king discovering my mother's empty home. How upset and distraught he'd seemed. Part of me wanted to confess everything right now, but I knew it was the desire of a child. I was still a dhampir who'd just left a cell in the Tower. Even if the king couldn't bring himself to execute his own daughter, all he had to do was lock the door and leave me there to rot.

"Why not resume the relationship after the queen's death?"

"I tried. Sadly, I couldn't find her, although the circumstances weren't much changed. I wouldn't have been able to marry her and I doubt she would've been content to continue as a concubine. It didn't suit her personality."

"Understandable." I couldn't imagine lurking in the shadows and awaiting my private audience with the king. It had to have been humiliating for her.

His gaze flicked to me. "The prince is in much the same position, you see."

I smiled. "Prince Maeron isn't lacking the adoration of female vampires. He's spoiled for choice. That's the real problem. He needs to have his heart broken a couple times."

The king gave me a pointed look. "I'm not talking about Maeron."

Oh. Right. "May I speak freely, Your Majesty?"

"Please."

"I have no interest in marriage, not to anyone, including a royal vampire."

"Good. Because it isn't possible and I like you. I would hate to see you disappointed."

"Hard to be disappointed when you have no expectations, Your Majesty."

We arrived at the gate and he motioned for the guards to let us pass.

"You don't dream of a brood of children? I would've loved a few more, but Imogen fell ill after Davina and the healers advised her to stop there."

"More often than not, I dream of a brood of monsters."

His mouth turned up at the corners. "There are potions to help with that."

"No thanks. I like the reminder. Wouldn't want to grow complacent."

The king gave me an appraising look. "I have enjoyed our chat, London."

"Me, too, Your Majesty. More than you know."

7

Once safely outside the Tower, I allowed myself a deep breath. I hadn't realized how much tension my body was holding until now. That whole affair could've easily gone sideways—well, more sideways than it did. Cynthia was dead, the Immortality Stone was missing, Maeron had solid leads on the fifth stone, and—worst of all —I was on the prince's radar again. My options for next steps were limited, which meant a change in plans. It was time to face my fears and seek help from someone who might want to see me dead.

I headed northwest on foot to a row of white terraced houses. All the buildings sported shiny black doors except for one. It might be a suicide mission, but if Maeron found me again, I'd be dead anyway.

I trudged up the steps and knocked on the glossy red door. I felt a surge of hope when I heard the lock shifting. The door swung open to reveal Adwin.

The royal winemaker seemed as surprised to see me as I was to see him. "Miss Hayes. Come in." He stepped aside and I slipped past him.

"I'm sorry to show up without an appointment or whatever the protocol is. Is the prince here?"

"I'm afraid not. Is there something I can help you with?"

"I need to speak with him urgently. If you can tell me where he is, I'd be grateful."

Adwin hesitated. "He's not to be disturbed. Ever since he returned from a trip, he's been quite agitated. I don't suppose you know anything about that."

Agitated as in *my return journey was filled with minor inconveniences* or agitated as in *I'm so upset I have to execute the woman I have the hots for*? Probably not a question for Adwin.

"Nothing I'm at liberty to share," I said.

He nodded. "Would you like a drink? Perhaps a nibble of something to eat?"

"Not today, thank you." I hated to refuse an offer of food from the royal pantry, but my stomach was tied in too many knots to digest food right now. "Why are you at the townhouse?"

"Callan and I were finalizing our presentation."

My eyebrows inched up. "For the synthetic blood proposal?"

He nodded. "We're planning a presentation for the king and queen next week."

"What about Maeron and Davina?"

"His Highness requested a private meeting to start with. He's concerned that Prince Maeron might…"

I held up a hand. "No need to explain. At this point I've had enough encounters with the prince to understand. Anyway, it's wonderful news. You must be nervous."

He smiled and showed off his neatly filed fangs. "Incredibly. The prince won't lose his head for the proposal, but it doesn't mean I won't lose mine."

I understood the feeling all too well. "The prince must feel confident that it will go well. Otherwise, he'd be reluctant to put you in a vulnerable position."

Adwin nodded. "Agreed. You know him well, Miss Hayes."

That was the issue. Callan gave me the chance to know him well. He let me in and I rewarded him with lies and deception. I couldn't blame him for leaving.

"Not well enough to know where he is this minute. Care to tell me where I might find him?"

"At the old churchyard tying up a few loose ends."

I'd discovered the old churchyard by accident. It was the secret location where Callan and Adwin had been meeting to discuss and develop their synthetic blood. It was ideal for showing my face to Callan. Maeron didn't know the place existed so he wouldn't look for me there.

"I hope you're able to raise his spirits," Adwin continued. "He's been so unlike himself. If it weren't for our joint project, I'd be avoiding him completely."

The information didn't make me feel better about going to see him.

"I'll be sure to tread lightly."

Adwin gave me an encouraging smile. "If anyone can sort him out, it's you, Miss Hayes. The two of you seem to have a special connection."

There was no point in arguing. "Thank you, Adwin. I'll show myself out."

I turned invisible in the foyer of the townhouse and left. If Maeron expected me to go running to Callan next, he'd have eyes on this place by now.

The old churchyard was only a short distance from the palace, which meant a bus ride from my current location. I leaned my head against the window as we rode through

Holborn and Covent Garden. If Callan and Adwin's plan succeeded, then synthetic blood would soon replace vampires' need for human blood. No more tribute centers. No more viewing humans as a food source. I knew it wouldn't be an easy sell for them, even if the formula was perfect. Vampires liked being at the top of the food chain and were set in their ways. The switch to synthetic blood might be regarded as a weakness by certain Houses, too, which opened the door for future conflict. I was curious how Casek would react to the proposal. He was still traditional enough to view an interspecies marriage as impossible, so there was every chance he'd reject the idea—or at least take time to consider it. Imogen seemed like she might hold fast to old ideas as well. Those in positions of power tended to avoid relinquishing any, hence the reason magic was still illegal. Vampires seemed to think the only way to rule was to oppress. Equality was too threatening.

I departed the bus and turned invisible again as I walked to the churchyard. A bird flew low overhead and I glanced up hoping to see Barnaby, but it was just a gray pigeon. I reached out with my mind to see whether I felt the raven's presence nearby. He'd done well at the Tower. I looked forward to thanking him.

I entered through the broken gate at the churchyard. There was no sign of the butterfly patrol that sometimes breezed through on Callan's behalf. Hopefully they weren't scheduled to arrive soon. This reunion demanded absolute privacy.

I waited until I was indoors to materialize. The interior was steeped in darkness. Feeling my way, I crept down the staircase to the underground lair. I reached the bottom and ground to a halt. Light emanated from a single torch on the wall, illuminating a shirtless Callan across the room. His skin gave the illusion of being sun-kissed and the muscles in his back rippled as he stacked barrels. I opened my mouth to speak but found my throat was too dry.

Sensing my presence, he twisted to look at me. His expression didn't change. Slowly, he set down the barrel in his hands and turned to face me. The front view was even better. Broad chest. Wide shoulders. Sculpted arms and torso. I'd taken such pains to block him from my mind that the sight of him in the flesh was more overwhelming than I'd anticipated.

"London," he said. His voice was barely a whisper.

"Callan."

"What are you doing here?" he asked.

"You're skipping over the part where I'm still alive." As much as I wanted to be closer, I maintained my distance.

He looked me over. "You look well. What happened to you?"

"Does it matter?"

He took a step closer. "To me? Yes."

He was close enough now that I smelled the musky scent of his body. It should've been a repellent. Instead it acted as a magnet, drawing me closer to him.

"You left. Shit happened. I made it home without you."

"I didn't leave you. I came back to apologize, but you were already gone. I searched for you. I found Fenella..."

"Fenella and Murdina betrayed us."

Anger sparked in his green eyes. "Betrayed us? How?"

"How do you think? There were vampires waiting for me when I reached the mainland. Murdina seemed downright giddy to turn me in. I guess I didn't express enough enthusiasm about the meal she made for us."

His jaw clicked. "She handed you over to my father?"

"Yep. And he was kind enough to imprison me in an

anti-magic tower. I only escaped because..." Okay, technically I didn't escape. Cynthia and Glendon plotted the whole thing together. I shook my head. "It's a long story."

He took another step toward me. "And I want to hear every word of it."

"Are you sure about that? I am your natural enemy, after all."

His expression softened. "I've thought of very little else since I left Skye." He suddenly snapped to attention. "Did my father take the Spirit Stone?"

"No. Fenella came to her senses and hid it for me until I was able to retrieve it."

His fingers twitched as though he was resisting the urge to touch me. I recognized it because I felt exactly the same.

"I am truly sorry. If I had realized what would happen..."

I waved him off. "I survived. There's something else you need to know."

"Something else?" He laughed. "What else can there possibly be?"

"Maeron has the Immortality Stone."

"What do you mean? It's in the Tower."

"Not anymore." I told him about the incident with Cynthia.

He raked a hand through his dark blond hair. "And you believe he's working with my father?"

"Is. Was. I'm not sure what the status is now. Whatever it is, he was very smug about it."

Callan chuckled. "I'm convinced Maeron was born smug."

"He's determined to get his hands on the other stones. He knows I have them."

"You mean the Spirit Stone."

It was time to come squeaky clean. "And the Elemental Stone." I paused. "And the Transcendence Stone."

"*You* have three stones?"

I squared my shoulders. "I do."

"What do you intend to do with them."

"Hide them."

"Hide them?" The words were cold enough to make me shiver.

"Yes."

He flinched. "From me?"

"From everyone."

"So I trust you, but you don't trust me. Does that about sum it up?"

"It isn't that I don't trust you. If I didn't, I wouldn't be here now."

"You're here because you're desperate, London, not because you trust me."

I hated that he was right.

"There's one more small detail you should know."

He blew out a laughing breath. "Let me guess. You're working for my father. No, wait. You're part of a secret organization whose primary goal is to remove vampires from power."

"Not quite." I told him about my mother and King Casek.

He looked for the nearest barrel and sat. "You're telling me that you're the daughter of the king? And that Maeron and Davina are your half siblings?"

"That's right. Do you need your smelling salts or do you think you can remain upright?"

He ignored my sarcasm. "You're a member of House Lewis."

"No. Not a vampire, remember? A dhampir. Illegal." I

pretended to slice across my neck. "Are you going to have me arrested?"

His head jerked toward me. "Do you really need to ask that question?"

I looked into his eyes and saw the answer. "I'm sorry, Callan. I'm sorry I believed the worst of you."

He rubbed his rugged jawline. "I didn't know what to do when I went back and you were gone. I assumed you'd simply continued without me."

"That was the plan, but obviously it didn't work out that way."

He shook his head. "By the devil, London. I wish you'd told me everything sooner."

"Put yourself in my shoes for a minute," I said. "You're a vampire. A *royal* vampire. My very existence is illegal—yet you expected me to confess everything?"

"I expected honesty. I shared my true self with you. Birmingham. Devon. I crossed into House Duncan territory to find you. Do you know how difficult that was for me?"

"I do."

His expression grew pained. "But it wasn't enough for you."

"Your 'enough' is different from mine. Even with your problems, you live in a world of endless money and opportunity and privilege." I pointed to myself. "I live in a world of oppression and fear. Sometimes those worlds intersect, but they're fundamentally different."

"And I'm to blame?"

"Of course not, but that doesn't change the fact that you benefit and I struggle. I hide and I lie because I'm forced to."

He gestured to the barrels around us. "Can't you see I'm trying to be the change I want to see in the world?"

My breath caught in my throat. My mother used to say that. It was one of the reasons I became a knight.

"And I think it's incredibly brave."

"But not enough for you?"

"It's not that simple, Callan."

He nodded. "Okay then. What can I say to convince you to trust me?"

"Nothing," I said quietly. "I had to get there on my own."

Hope lit up his green eyes. "Had?"

I took a step forward. "I'm there, Callan." I frowned. "Or here. I'm here."

The moment stretched and we stared at each other.

"Is that everything?" he asked.

I splayed my hands. "That's everything. If there's more, it's only because I don't know it yet."

He now knew more about me than anyone else, including Kami. I felt like I'd stripped naked. The feeling was both uncomfortable and liberating.

He moved with preternatural speed. One second he sat on the barrel and the next his powerful arms engulfed me.

"Kiss me or kill me. Up to you," I said.

His mouth sought mine. Kiss it is then.

"I'm glad you're okay," he murmured.

"I bet you would've felt pretty guilty otherwise."

I pressed my cheek against his bare chest and listened to the thumping of his heart. Intense and steady like the vampire himself.

He kissed me like he needed my lips to survive. "I don't deserve you," he whispered.

I pulled back to look at him. "And here I thought I was the bad egg."

"Your work as a knight is valiant, London. It has meaning. I've done terrible things for terrible reasons."

I stood on my tiptoes and planted another kiss on his lips. "All in the past. That's not the vampire you are anymore." I didn't think it ever truly was.

He slid his fingers through my hair. "If my brother lays a single manicured nail on you, I'll kill him with my bare hands."

"Don't."

He inclined his head. "Don't?"

"Think about twelve-year-old you."

"Maeron is far from twelve, London. He's an adult."

"I know, but inside him is an angry little boy. He lost his mother at a young age. I think he feels as lost now as he did then and the end result is bad decision-making."

"He has a family who loves him. Davina adores him."

"It isn't that simple."

"What do you suggest then? I let him kill you and acquire the stones to rule the world alongside my miserable father because he couldn't get past his suffering?"

"Of course not, but I think he's in over his head. Your father will chew him up, spit him out, and pick his teeth with Maeron's bones, only Maeron doesn't know it yet."

"You think I should confront him?"

"Whatever you do, it needs to be quick. He has a team working around the clock in search of the fifth stone. They think it contains summoning powers and I suspect they're right."

"How did he determine that?"

"Research. He even commandeered the library to do it."

Callan's mouth twitched. "I didn't think Maeron knew the library's address."

"He probably doesn't."

He cupped the back of my head. "What about you?"

"That depends on how your conversation goes. He wants

the other three stones. He knows I have them. He won't leave me alone until he gets them."

"We need to get to that fifth stone before he does."

"And before your father. If Glendon sent Cynthia for the Immortality Stone, I'd bet anything he's got his own team hunting for the final one."

"My father is a far worse threat than Maeron."

"Maybe for you. They've both imprisoned me, although Maeron didn't manage to hold me more than ten minutes, bless him. Top marks for effort though."

Callan's face turned to stone. "My brother is a fool. My father will kill him once he gets what he wants."

"I don't doubt it. There was a distinct chill in the air every time I was in a room with him."

He studied me. "Not too often, I hope."

"You walk like him."

He grunted. "I hope that's the only resemblance. The best thing that ever happened to me was that treaty."

"Because it brought you to a new family?"

In a tender move that surprised me, he leaned down to kiss my forehead. "And you, London. Because it brought me to you."

8

After my reunion with Callan, I returned to the bakery to wash off the stench of failure and regroup. When I emerged from the bathroom, Mack stood at the pinball machine in the midst of an intense game. He turned to look at the towel wrapped around my head.

"I have to admit, I didn't quite think it through when I offered up my man cave."

"If you're desperate for fun and games, have at it. I can dry my hair in the bathroom."

"I'm not here for fun and games." He released his grip on the machine and pivoted to face me. "Your friend is missing. The mouthy one."

"Kami?"

He nodded. "No one from your banner could get in touch with you. The cranky one decided to call me."

"Minka?"

"Uptight. Prissy. Could probably turn a hunk of coal into a diamond if we positioned it right."

"Do you have descriptive names for all the knights in my banner?"

He shrugged. "All except you. I haven't worked with any of the other ones." He ticked them off on his fingers. "There's also the sisters-who-aren't-twins, the sweetheart, and the water witch."

My mind returned to Kami. "Why does Minka think she's missing?"

"You'd have to ask her. It was urgent enough that she called repeatedly until I answered." He scratched his head. "Is she always that high-pitched?"

"When she's stressed."

"In other words, yes. Where's your phone?"

"Charging." I crossed the room and unplugged the phone where it had been resting on the Ping-Pong table. I removed the towel from my head and slung it over my shoulder.

Minka picked up on the first ring. "London, thank the gods. Is Kami with you?"

"No. Why do you think she's missing?"

"She was supposed to meet Neera and Ione at the market, but she didn't show up and no one can reach her. She would never miss out on kebabs."

"When's the last time anyone heard from her?"

"Last night," Minka said. "She spoke to Stevie. How about you?"

"This morning."

"Where was she?"

Nausea rolled over me. "I need to go."

"London, wait..."

I hung up and spun to face Mack. "Maeron has her."

Mack blanched. "The prince took the mouthy one? Why?"

"He needed leverage." And I'd basically tied a bow

around her and left her as a gift on the doorstep of the Tower. Smooth move, London.

"Why hasn't he contacted you then? It won't work if you don't know he has her."

"He doesn't know how to find me. He's been waiting for me to make the discovery."

Mack pressed his fingertips to his temples and groaned. "Listen, I want to help you, but vampires are my bread and butter. If I piss off House Lewis..."

"I know, Mack."

"We can't all survive on integrity and self-respect."

I smiled at him. "I know. It's okay. This is my fight. I don't expect you to help me."

I didn't bother to tell him the real stakes. It would only make him feel guilty. He had a family to feed. Sure, I had the menagerie, but they were taken care of right now. If something happened to me, they were in good hands. I couldn't say the same for Mack's family.

He gave one more exasperated grunt for good measure. "If you need any weapons, feel free to borrow."

"I have what I need, thanks."

Mack seemed reluctant to leave. "Do you know where he wants you to go?"

"I have an idea."

He nodded. "Good luck, London. Next time I come back here, you and I are playing another round of pinball. I need to reclaim my championship title."

"Deal."

I shut the door behind him and got myself ready. I sheathed Babe and secured Bert and Ernie. It was a good thing I'd released magic in the shower because I was going to need to maintain complete control when I saw my brother again. It was one thing to mess with me. It was quite another to mess with my best friend.

Ezra glanced up from the counter on my way out. "Everything good?"

"Not really. Some moron decided it would be a good idea to hold Kami hostage."

Ezra tossed me a scone. "Give him hell, London."

I tucked the scone into my pocket for later. "That's the plan."

I left the bakery and didn't bother to turn invisible. There was no point. Maeron was waiting for me. It was just a question of where. Since he couldn't contact me directly, he'd want to make it easy for me to find them. His best chance was to hold Kami hostage at a familiar place, which gave me two options and luckily both were in the same neighborhood. The first one was the library, which was still 'under construction.' The second one was my flat, which he likely knew was unoccupied.

I decided to start with my flat for no other reason than I wanted to see it.

The building was quiet when I entered, which wasn't unusual. The tenants were older and kept to themselves. One of the reasons I'd chosen to live here was because of its tucked-away location near Euston Station. It wasn't a block that got too much attention from the authorities or anyone else.

I crept up the staircase to the top floor. The door was unlocked and the ward still broken. I nudged open the door and peered inside. I expected to find a mess from when Maeron's men ransacked the place, but someone must've cleaned up for me. All the furniture was back in its original position and the floor was clean—relatively speaking.

I checked the kitchen first. Nothing seemed out of place.

The bathroom was fine except for a broken towel rail. The bedroom was intact.

No Kami.

I opened the window to check the makeshift balcony. There was no sign that anyone had been there. I closed the window and locked it.

I took a moment to linger. I didn't realize how much I missed my flat until I was standing in the middle of it. I pictured Jemima pecking the leg of the wardrobe while her diaper sagged off her feathered bottom. The bantam hen seemed to take her aggression out on the wood furniture. I imagined Hera curled up on my pillow. She loved to leave cat hair in places where I sat or slept. I was sure it was deliberate.

I breathed a sigh. I'd be back and when I was, the menagerie would be with me. We'd be a family again.

I reached the landing on the second floor as a door opened a crack. A face peered through the small gap. I didn't know the tenant's name, but apparently he knew mine.

"Is that you, London Hayes?"

I stopped to look back at him. "There's no point in reporting that you saw me. You won't get the reward money."

A pause. "Why not?"

"Because I'm on my way to see the one who offered to pay."

The door slammed shut.

Shaking my head, I left the building. It shouldn't have surprised me that Maeron had offered a reward to my neighbors. All the tenants were in need of money. Hell, I should have reported a sighting myself and collected the reward.

I listened to the noises of the city as I walked to the

library. Horns honked. Voices raised. It had been so quiet in Scotland. It would've been downright peaceful if not for the whole stress of imprisonment.

Maeron was a fool if he thought I'd hand over the stones. If he wanted them badly enough, he'd have to figure out a way to summon them from my pocket dimension. Good luck with that.

So far I'd managed to avoid worrying too much about Kami. She was tough and Maeron had no reason to hurt her...yet. The real danger would emerge once I was there and refused to cooperate.

The sign outside indicated the library was still closed. The door, however, was ajar. I accepted the invitation to enter. Kami was here. I felt it in my bones.

There was no sign of Pedro or anyone else. No minions waited in the shadows to jump me. Good. That meant the only one I had to hurt was Maeron.

I paused to listen for any sounds of struggle. My efforts were met with silence.

I arrived at the Reading Room and folded my arms. "I heard a package of mine was delivered here by mistake."

Maeron sat with his feet up on one of the curved tables and his fingers slotted behind his head. Kami sat across from him, bound to a chair in anti-magic chains. He'd gagged her, too, not that I blamed him. She would've scorched his ears with her salty language.

Kami's blue eyes narrowed when she noticed me. I couldn't tell whether she was angry I took so long or judging my outfit.

I motioned between them. "I didn't know you two were friends."

"Come in, London. We've been expecting you." He grinned at his hostage. "Haven't we, Kamikaze?"

I started toward them, maintaining a casual air. "Let me get this straight. I helped rescue your kidnapped sister and, in return, you kidnap my best friend. Doesn't seem very sporting of you, Your Highness."

"Give me the stones or your friend dies. Is that sporting enough for you?"

Despite the gag, Kami groaned and rolled her eyes.

Maeron glared at her before returning his attention to me.

"You offered to pay my neighbors to spy on me," I said. "Pretty unscrupulous."

"Scruples have nothing to do with it. I'm the prince of House Lewis. I have a right to know everything that happens within my borders."

"So if I see someone litter, I should report that directly to you?" I tugged my phone from my pocket. "In that case, let me make a note of your number."

He shifted his feet to the floor and stood. "My spies are everywhere. There's nowhere in the realm you can go where you'd be safe from me." He met my gaze. "Make no mistake. That is a threat, Miss Hayes."

I put away my phone. "Noted. Still not giving you the stones."

He strode toward me. "You will when I break every bone in your body and you beg for mercy."

His hand shot out and grabbed my neck. My magic flared in response and I *pushed*. The vampire slid backward, but he managed to stay on his feet. I whipped out both daggers and flung them at the same time. The blades snagged Maeron's sleeves and pinned him to a column in the middle of the room.

I ran to Kami and ripped off the gag.

Maeron tore his jacket in his attempt to free himself.

"You'll pay for that. This jacket is bespoke. I designed it myself."

"You're very talented," I told him.

Kami squinted.

I gave her an innocent look. "What? It's a nice jacket."

Kami stood and held out her wrists. I unsheathed Babe. I gave the chains a good whack.

"I don't think so." Maeron advanced.

I used my free hand to command a gust of air. I didn't have to hurt Maeron. I only had to keep him at bay long enough to free Kami.

He blasted backward and crashed into a table and chairs. "Need I remind you the penalty for illegal use of magic is death," he said as he struggled to his feet.

I whacked the chains again and they broke. Kami shook off the remainder of metal. Magic sparked in her blue eyes.

"He's mine, London."

Maeron only managed two steps toward us when his body went rigid.

"Leave us alone," Kami ordered. I didn't think I'd ever seen her as angry as she looked right now.

Beads of sweat pilled across the prince's brow. "You won't break me," he said through gritted teeth. "We train for witches like you."

I didn't doubt it.

Kami retrieved my daggers and held one of the sharp blades to Maeron's neck. "I don't care who you are. This has to stop."

I thrust my hands forward. "Kami, wait! You can't."

"What choice do we have? He won't quit until you're dead and I refuse to let that happen." She dragged the blade along his skin. "Or I can make him do it himself. No one will know what really happened."

"He won't kill me, Kami. Not while I have what he wants."

"And what about after that? What's to stop him then?" Kami pressed the blade deeper into his skin until crimson bubbles rose to the surface. "Callan may be hot for you, but his loyalty is to his family, not you."

My eyes locked with Maeron's. It was a gamble, but Kami was right. Maeron was stubborn and relentless like his mother and I was out of options.

"There's something you need to know," I said.

"There is nothing you can tell me that's going to change my mind. Prince or no prince, I won't let him hurt you."

"He isn't going to hurt me." I drew a deep breath and sheathed Babe. "He's my brother."

Laughter erupted from Kami. "Nice one, London."

"I'm serious." I lowered my hands in an effort to convince Kami to lower the dagger.

She stared at me in disbelief as the truth registered. "How?"

"My mother and his father fell in love."

She shook her head in an effort to process the information. "Your mother fell in love with a vampire? No, not just a vampire. The king of House Lewis?"

"Yes."

Kami released her hold on him.

Maeron stumbled forward before finding his feet. "Why would you concoct such a preposterous story? Do you truly think it will save you from your fate?"

Kami raised the dagger, but I urged her to lower it again.

"My mother worked briefly at the palace," I said. "She met your father there and they fell in love."

Maeron went slack-jawed. "That's absurd."

"My mother's name was Rhea." I didn't know what

surname she would've used then. I'd already come to the realization that she'd changed it when she left him. Otherwise it would've been too easy for the king to find her. "Mention that name in front of your father and see how he reacts."

Maeron's nostrils flared. "And where is this seductress now?"

"Dead. She's been dead for years. She never told me the name of my father, only that he was a vampire."

"You're trying to persuade me that my father chose a common witch over Queen Britannia herself?" He laughed but the sound rang hollow in my ears.

"I'm not trying to persuade you of anything. I'm simply telling you what I learned at the Atheneum."

"Lies," he seethed.

"If I'm lying, then why did I not let Kami kill you?"

"Because of the repercussions, of course."

I laughed. "Letting you live after she tried to kill you is going to have fewer repercussions?"

Uncertainty flickered in his brown eyes. Without another word, he transformed into a butterfly and flew away.

Kami raised the dagger. "I'm a good shot. I can still hit him."

I placed a hand on her arm. "Don't."

She dropped her hand to her side and faced me. "Is it true?"

I nodded.

"I can't believe it."

"Trust me. It took me a little time as well."

She licked her lips. "Who else knows?"

"Callan, but that's it."

She laughed bitterly. "That's it? The Demon of House

Duncan knows you're a dhampir and you act like he found out you're a vegetarian."

"He already knows I'm a vegetarian."

Her expression grew pained. "And now the vile prince of House Lewis knows you're a dhampir, too."

"He also knows I'm his sister."

Kami stared at the space vacated by Maeron. "Do you think that matters to him?"

I thought of his fondness for Davina. "I hope so. It's the only card I have left to play." The stones didn't count. There wasn't enough leverage in the world to make me turn them over to a vampire.

Out of the corner, something moved. I snatched a dagger from Kami's hand and raised it to throw.

"No. Don't shoot...or throw." Pedro crawled out from under a table. "Is it over?"

I relaxed and hurried over to help the librarian to his feet. "Pedro, how long have you been stuck there?"

He shrugged. "Let's just say I need to change my trousers."

Well, he was alive. That was the important thing.

Unfortunately, the map and all the research were gone.

I sighed. "Looks like Maeron was smart enough to cover his tracks this time."

Pedro glanced at the empty table. "If you want to know where he sent his teams, I can tell you that."

"Teams, plural?"

He nodded. "Northumberland, Cumbria and Durham."

The same three locations they'd been investigating. They must have reached a wall in their research and decided to go anyway. Maeron seemed the type to act out of desperation.

"They're taking trains north today," Pedro continued.

That didn't give us much time. "Thank you, Pedro. I think that's the most important fact you've ever given me."

Kami tugged my shirt. "Stop fawning over the librarian and let's go."

"Is it true what you said?" Pedro asked, adjusting his crumpled shirt. "Are you the king's daughter?"

I nodded.

He gazed at me in wonder. "Wow."

I clapped his arm. "I'd love to stay and chat, but we're sort of under the gun."

He flicked his fingers. "Go. Save the...whatever it is."

"Call the banner," I told Kami as we exited the library. "Tell everyone to meet at the Pavilion ASAP. We have an urgent situation."

Kami cast me a sidelong glance. "You're not going to try to handle this one on your own?"

"Not this time. The stone isn't a 'me' problem. It's a 'we' problem."

"Don't you get it, London? Anything that's a 'you' problem is an 'us' problem. That's what it means to have people who care about you."

Barnaby appeared overhead and I nearly choked with relief. A small part of me worried that Maeron had captured him, too. The raven flew low enough for me to reach out and touch his feathers.

"You had me scared for a minute, bud."

"Now you know how the rest of us feel all the time," Kami said.

"We're headed north," I told Barnaby. "Maeron sent teams to recover the stone, so our team is preparing to do the same."

The raven cawed and flew away.

Kami smiled at me.

I peered at her. "What?"

She bumped me with her shoulder. "You said our team."

"Because we *are* a team."

"I know, but it's nice to hear you acknowledge it. You're not alone, no matter how much you want to be."

I gave her a sad smile. "I don't want to be alone, Kami. I never did."

9

T rio was the first to greet me at the Pavilion. The three-headed dog rushed forward before I made it to my desk. Acidic slobber dripped from all three mouths.

"I've missed you, too," I said, rubbing the center head. "Sounds like you've been doing a good job here."

"Who's the best security dog? Who is she?" Kami nuzzled the dog's faces. "That's right. You are."

Briar strolled into the room eating a bag of nuts. Her wild red hair was in desperate need of a haircut. When her gaze landed on me, the bag dropped to the floor and she ran over to hug me.

"I'm so happy to see you."

Trio got to the nuts faster than Briar could retrieve them.

"Worth it," she said, smiling. "I take it you're the emergency."

"Not quite. I'll explain once everyone's here."

Neera strode in next, along with Ione. Tall and slender with their light brown hair in matching French twists, they really did look more like twins than plain, old sisters. Relief shone in their eyes at the sight of me.

"Stevie said you were back. Glad you're safe." Neera clapped my shoulder.

"Heard about the sepa demons," Ione added. "I was sorry I missed it."

"You wouldn't say that if you'd been there," Kami said. "They were disgusting."

"Kamikaze, thank the gods." Minka hurried into the room. "Where were you?"

"At the library," Kami said.

Minka scowled. "All that worry and you were at the library?" She paused. "Since when do you read?"

"It's why we've called this meeting," I said.

Briar frowned. "Because Kami's decided to embrace reading?"

"Wait. We still need Stevie," Minka said. She scattered papers on her desk. "Here. Fill out these incident reports while we're waiting."

Kami and I exchanged looks as Minka handed each of us a form to complete.

Stevie entered the room, prompting a sigh of relief from Kami. She tossed the form onto her desk.

"We're all present and accounted for," Kami announced. "We can start."

Minka sat behind her desk and uncapped a pen. "I'll take notes."

"Why don't you listen first?" I suggested. "If you want to jot down notes later, feel free."

Minka set down her pen and gave us her full attention.

"There are things you deserve to hear from me," I began. The truth was still hard to share. Maybe with time and practice, it would get easier.

I hoped.

The women stared at me in stunned silence—all except

Kami, who was busy tossing treats into Trio's three mouths. She seemed to be working out a pattern.

"You're King Casek's daughter," Minka said for the third time.

"It doesn't get any more or less true when you repeat it," Neera advised.

"And both the princes know?" Briar asked. "Doesn't that worry you?"

"A lot of things worry me," I said. "The floating island of garbage in the ocean that even the Great Eruption failed to destroy. The cat insists on peeing in the bathtub when she's mad at me. The fact that red food dye stains my teeth." I shrugged.

"The priority is the stone," Kami said.

I nodded. "And right now Maeron has his minions heading north to find the final one."

"Then we need to beat them there," Stevie said.

Minka shushed her. "Let her finish."

"They're headed to Cumbria, Northumberland, and Durham. I don't know if they've uncovered more information since then, but I don't think so."

"I've never been that far north," Neera said.

Minka adopted a smug expression. "I have."

"Good, then you can act as a guide," Kami told her.

Minka recoiled. "Oh no. I can't go with you. Somebody needs to stay here. It'll be suspicious if all the knights in the banner disappear at once."

She wasn't wrong. On the other hand, we might need every capable knight at our disposal to find the stone before Maeron. Just because Minka preferred to sit behind a desk didn't mean she lacked useful skills.

"If you're staying behind, then you'll have to be in charge of the menagerie," I said.

She froze. "All of them?"

I splayed my hands. "I don't see another option, do you?"

"I know someone who can help," Briar said. "There's a wizard in my building named Oscar. He runs a rescue."

Minka's browed creased. "He runs a rescue out of his flat?"

She nodded. "He doesn't usually offer doggie daycare-type services, but he would as a favor to me."

"I've seen your flat," Neera said. "If his is anywhere close to that size, I don't see how he can take on all those extra animals if he's already operating a rescue."

"He has summoning powers," Briar explained. "He sends the rescues to another plane for safekeeping until he can find them homes."

"That sounds dangerous," Minka said. "What if he gets caught using magic and the animals get trapped there?"

"He's been doing this for years," Briar said. "He only uses magic at home so there's very little chance of being caught."

"I'm sure the menagerie will be fine there." They were accustomed to being transported to another dimension.

"You're not worried about them coping in a strange environment?" Ione asked. "We don't know anything about the alternate plane. What if there are monsters there?"

"Depends on whether he accessed it or created it himself," I said.

Ione laughed. "Created it? I don't think that's even possible. He's a wizard not a god."

I swallowed the lump in my throat. Time for another bombshell. "If I can do it, there's a chance he can, too."

All heads swiveled to face me.

"Could you repeat that?" Minka asked.

Kami cut her a sideways glance. "Why? So you can repeat it three more times afterward?"

Neera crossed her arms and leveled me with a look. "If we're going to put our lives on the line, then you need to tell us everything, London. Not just the parts you think we need to know. Everything."

Ione offered a firm nod. "Neera's right. You've been treating us like children."

"She's not treating you like children," Kami interrupted. "She's treating you like family she wants to protect and you should consider yourselves lucky."

Minka spread her arms. "There's no need to argue. We're all on the same team."

Neera handed me a marker. "Tell us about the stone. And don't leave anything out."

I squinted at the hot pink marker. "Don't we have a more solemn color? I feel like black is more appropriate."

"They all dried out and we don't have money in the budget for more until next quarter," Minka explained.

"Hot pink it is." I stood at the whiteboard and drew a picture of Friseal's Temple.

"Are we going to Egypt?" Ione asked.

Kami shushed her.

Ione blinked. "What? It looks like a pyramid."

"Pyramid. Tower. Ziggurat. It's all the same," I said. "The point is five of these stones survived and four of them have been recovered. Maeron is on the hunt for the fifth one that I'm calling the Summoning Stone." I explained how the stones might influence those with related abilities.

"Thankfully none of us has summoning abilities except London," Minka said.

"What happened when you were near the Transcendence Stone?" Stevie asked.

I popped the lid on the marker. "I was able to create multiple versions of myself."

Ione burst into laughter. "What? Like clones?"

"Not exactly. They're all pieces of me, with all the same abilities."

"But if one dies...?" Minka asked.

"I don't die," I said. At least I didn't think so. As far as I knew, none of my multiples had been killed. They just...dissipated.

Ione leaned forward and rested her chin on her fists. "What else can you do?"

"The point of this discussion is the Summoning Stone," I reminded her.

"No, the point of this discussion is how we can obtain the stone without dying," Neera said.

"If we're in a race, shouldn't we be running to a train?" Briar asked.

Stevie perked up. "Can you portal us there, London?"

I shook my head. "I don't have all the summoning skills. I wish I did, though. It would've made my recent trips easier." Although I would've missed out on time with Callan.

"There's no way we can beat Maeron's men if they've already left," Neera pointed out.

I turned toward her. "It just so happens I know a guy."

"We know lots of guys," Kami said. "What's so special about this one?"

"Come with me and find out."

JOSEPH YARDLEY GAPED at me like I had three heads and the horn of a narwhal. "You want me to teleport all these people?"

I'd brought the knights to the place where the People in Support of Ra held their secret meetings. Even without the secret password for admission, the bouncers took one look at our weapons and let us pass.

"Not all at once," I told the Green Wizard. "We're not going to the same place. We've split into three teams." I pointed to each group. "Cumbria, Durham, Northumberland."

Yardley chuckled lightly like I'd told him a dad joke. His chuckle slowly morphed into full-blown laughter until he was doubled over.

Annoyance flickered across Kami's face. "If you can't do it, just say so."

"I can't do it," he said between fits of laughter.

"Do you know anyone who can?" I asked.

His smile faded and he straightened. "You're serious."

"If I say the fate of the world depends on it, will you laugh again?"

His eyes sparkled with interest. "Is it a stone?"

There was no point in hiding the truth at this point. If I wanted Yardley on my side, I had to give him a reason to trust me. "Yes."

"I don't suppose you'll donate it to the cause once you have it."

"I don't think these stones can bring back the sun," I said. "I'm sorry."

Kami popped a hand on her hip. "Unless you want the vampires to control a stone that can control you..."

He spun toward me. "It's a Summoner Stone?"

"I've been calling it the Summoning Stone, but yes. We think so."

"If that stone is anywhere near as powerful as the Elemental Stone..." He pressed his lips together. "There are other summoners in this group. Perhaps together we can generate enough energy to get you there."

"Are they coming to the meeting?"

He nodded. "Members should start arriving any minute."

"I was hoping you'd say that."

Yardley directed us to a large table at the back of the room where we could discuss the plan in greater depth.

"My abilities only operate in this realm," he explained. "I can't access other planes of existence. If you want to teleport to Birmingham, fine. If you want to teleport to some unnamed dimension, you'd have to find a more skilled wizard."

Kami cringed. "Who would want to teleport to Birmingham?"

Stevie nudged me. "So his skill is the opposite of yours."

"Sort of."

"What about getting back?" Neera asked. "We don't want to be stranded in the north with Maeron's men."

Yardley shook his head. "We won't have the kind of energy required to hold a portal open indefinitely, nor can we open one for you to jump through later. Once you're there, you'll have to make your way back on your own."

"Assuming we..." Kami began.

I caught her gaze and shook my head. *Don't go there*, my face said.

She left the sentence unfinished.

Members filed into the room and Yardley snapped his fingers for their attention. All the attendees immediately focused on him.

"I wish you were as responsive to me," Minka grumbled.

"You tell us to sharpen our pencils," Kami whispered. "He's calling them to action."

"I don't see the difference."

Kami cut a glance at her. "And therein lies the problem."

Yardley gestured to us. "Our sisters-in-arms are here to request our assistance for a very important mission. I'd like to ask all my summoners to gather to the right of the room. Everyone else can go home."

Murmurs rippled through the crowd.

"This is a private operation," Yardley continued. "And we need to maintain focus. We can't do that with too many distractions milling around."

"What about the brownies?" someone called.

"You may each take a brownie home with you," he said.

Kami peered over his shoulder at the plates laden with baked goods. "Can I have a brownie for the road?"

I exhaled. "Who else wants a brownie before we get started?"

All hands shot up.

Kami ran over to the table to inspect the options. "Ooh, these have caramel."

I looked at Yardley. "I did mention the fate of the world hangs in the balance, didn't I?"

"I believe so." His expression turned solemn. "Once you're there, if you need reinforcements, don't hesitate to call. You have my number."

Kami bit into a brownie and moaned with pleasure. "Nobody is leaving this room without trying one."

Stevie scraped back her chair and stood. "If I'm going to die, might as well be with a brownie in my stomach."

Yardley directed his attention to the gathered summoners. "We might as well call the meeting to order so we can get started. All in favor of breaking the law?"

The summoners raised their hands. "Aye."

10

"I feel sick." Kami clutched her stomach.

I probably should've felt sorry for her, but I didn't. "I told you not to have that second brownie before teleporting."

I surveyed our new surroundings. Yardley teleported my team to Northumberland with the caveat that he couldn't necessarily deliver us to a precise location. I didn't have one anyway, so it worked out.

"At least we're outside," Briar said. "I was worried he'd teleport us into someone's loo."

"I was hoping he would." Kami sniffed her armpits. "I need a shower."

Briar tilted her head back to admire a gatehouse made of solid stone. "Maybe the Summoning Stone is in one of those walls."

I couldn't rule it out after my experience with the Transcendence Stone. That stone had been part of an estate for centuries before its discovery, which was mainly due to the owner's neglect of the building.

Kami shook her head. "We're not that lucky."

A woman walked toward us with her head down. She wore a handkerchief over her head, but tufts of auburn hair peeked out from the sides. Her burgundy coat was well-worn and she carried a flashlight that she kept aimed at the pavement.

I waved to get her attention. "Pardon me, ma'am. Can you tell me where we are?"

The woman glanced up and flinched. She seemed torn between stopping and breaking into a run. I understood the sentiment.

"We're not vampires," I assured her.

The woman swept the flashlight over us as though confirming my claim. "So I see." She eyed the structure behind us. "That's the gatehouse to what was once a castle. The castle's been gone for centuries, though, so you won't be seeing that."

I cast a glance over my shoulder at the gatehouse. "I meant the town."

She seemed confused by the question. "You're in Morpeth."

Well, we'd made it to the right county at least. Excellent work, Yardley.

I gestured to Kami and Briar. "We're knights from Britannia City and we're looking for information."

The woman cast a speculative glance at us. "What kind of information?"

"We're looking for an ancient artifact that could be somewhere in this area..."

"Ah, right. Then you should see the oracle."

"I'm not looking for a prophecy. I'm looking for a rock with markings."

"You should still see the oracle."

I sighed.

"Gee, a single-minded woman," Kami murmured. "I can't imagine who she reminds me of."

I forced a smile at the single-minded woman. "Fine. We'll see the oracle. Where is she?"

"Them," the woman said.

"Where is them?" Kami looked at me. "That isn't grammatically correct."

"Where are *they*?" I asked.

The woman pointed. "You'll want to go that way until you reach the Wyevale Christmas Shop and Beer Garden."

I looked at her expectantly. "And?"

"And that's where you'll find them."

"At the Christmas shop?"

The woman nodded. "And beer garden. That's right. Ask for Abby. Tell her Gwyneth sent you." The woman continued walking with her head bowed and her light aimed at the pavement.

Kami smiled. "A beer garden sounds good to me."

"Weren't you feeling unwell a scant two minutes ago?"

"I'm better now."

Briar snorted. "You two bicker like Ione and Neera. You might as well be sisters."

Kami started walking. "London has a real sister now. She doesn't need me to be her family."

My eyes widened. "Are you serious?" I fell in step with her. "Is that what you really think?"

Kami shrugged. "You adore Davina. You said that even before you knew she's your sister."

"Okay, but Davina doesn't know about me and, even if she did, that doesn't change the relationship I have with you."

Kami kept her gaze ahead. "It will. Why have a fake family when you have the option of a real one?"

I shot Briar a helpless look. "Kami, you and I have a history that no one can change. You're my best friend. You'll always be my best friend, no matter who else is in my life."

Kami stopped walking and pivoted to face me. "I don't have the option of another family. No secret sisters or unknown fathers. The knights are all I have. *You* are all I have."

I gripped her shoulders. "And nothing will change that. You're family to me. No shared blood required."

"What about me?" Briar asked. "Am I part of this?"

Kami tugged her closer to us and threw an arm across her shoulders. "I drifted for years before I became a knight. The banner gave me what I'd been missing from my life. A home, a purpose, and a family."

"And if it weren't for you, I never would've joined," I said.

"Group hug," Briar declared.

Kami smiled at me. "London isn't much of a hugger."

"I'll make an exception this once if it'll make you feel better." I stood with my arms at my sides.

Kami observed me. "You know that's not how hugs work, right? Generally you need to move your arms."

"Oh, I thought you were going to hug me." I opened my arms and Kami and Briar folded into them. I patted them each on the back. Briar, on the other hand, squeezed me like I was a near-empty tube of toothpaste.

"Too much," Kami croaked. She extricated herself from Briar's clutches. "Sheesh. And here I thought only your beast form was strong."

"Can we go now?" I asked. "Has everyone been appropriately reassured?"

"I'd like to be reassured that you'll let me have one drink at the beer garden," Kami said.

I ignored her and started walking. Morpeth was a

picturesque market town that seemed to have retained much of its character since the Eternal Night began. It was one of the lucky ones.

We found the Wyevale Christmas Shop and Beer Garden next to a secondhand clothing shop.

Briar sighed with pleasure. "I love Christmas."

The shop interior reeked of evergreen and cloves. The shelves were lined with scented candles, tree ornaments, and other assorted decorations. The wall at the back opened directly to the beer garden.

Kami regarded the riot of red and green inside the shop. "Beer and Christmas? Whose idea was this combo?"

"I think it's so that kids and adults have something to keep them occupied at the same time." Briar pointed to the sign to our right labeled 'Santa's Grotto.' "I've always called him Father Christmas."

"Probably too many letters for the sign," Kami said.

I followed their gazes. "I've never been in a grotto."

Kami shrugged. "You've lived in tunnels, so close enough."

A petite woman approached us with a ready smile. She wore a red dress with an apron overlay. "Can I help you, ladies? The beer garden doesn't open again for another half hour, but we have plenty to interest you in the shop in the meantime." She motioned to the axe strapped to my back. "I'm afraid we have a 'no weapons' policy. If you want to shop, you'll have to store them behind the counter until you've finished."

"We don't intend to shop. Are you Abby?" I asked.

She blinked. "I am."

"Gwyneth sent us."

"I see." She cast a furtive glance around the shop. "There

are no appointments, so now's a good time. Why don't you go right in?"

"In where?"

Abby motioned to the grotto.

Briar's eyes rounded. "Santa is our oracle?"

Abby shushed her. "We don't say the 'o' word out loud in the shop." She ushered us toward the grotto. "Go on then. There's a family due to arrive in thirty minutes, so you don't have much time."

Kami ducked inside first, and Briar followed next. I lowered my head and entered. The first thing that struck me was the change in temperature. It was freezing and I instinctively hugged myself.

The walls were designed to resemble a cave. Small lights lined the ceiling to imitate the look of stalactites. A throne-like chair was pushed against the wall with a stool on either side of it.

I glanced around the grotto. "How is it so cold in here? It's penetrating my magical armor."

Kami rubbed her arms. "I think the more important question is why is it so cold in here?"

"Because we're supposed to be at the North Pole, I think," Briar said.

The jingling of bells caught me off guard.

"Wrong," a voice bellowed. A rocky wall slid aside to reveal a stout man dressed in a red suit with a thick black belt. His white beard covered most of his face like a cloud of cotton. "If you had to wear this getup all day, you'd want a colder temperature too."

"It's mostly Marjorie's fault," another voice said. A young woman emerged in a green suit with a red belt and a pointy green hat. Her red shoes were the most ridiculous part of her ensemble. They curled up at the toes and were adorned with silver bells.

"I can't help my hot flashes," a third voice said. A brown-haired woman entered the grotto behind the other two. Her ensemble matched the younger woman's, except with the opposite color emphasis. "It gets too hot in here and then I can't focus. If I can't focus, I can't do my job." She fixed her hands on her hips and regarded us. "Who are you? I don't have anybody on the schedule for right now."

"I'm London and these are my companions from the Knights of Boudica."

"Boudica," Santa said. "Now there's a name I haven't heard in a long time."

"I take it you're not here for Santa," the young woman said.

"No. We're looking for the oracle."

"Thank Hecate." Santa ripped off the beard to reveal a pruned face.

Briar gasped. "Santa's a woman. I knew a man couldn't accomplish all those tasks in a single night."

Santa chuckled. "My name's Miriam. The elf with hot flashes is Marjorie and the one with the killer body is Meghan."

The killer body offered a friendly wave. "I do wish you'd stop objectifying me, Miriam."

"And I wish I still had a killer body." She shrugged. "This is how you know Santa isn't real."

"Have a seat. What brings you to the grotto?" Marjorie asked.

I looked for a chair and spotted two enormous beanbags on the floor—one red and one green. Kami and Briar squished together on the red one and I tried to settle grace-fully on the green one but to no avail. I sank into the fabric and worried I'd be stuck there forever. It didn't help that Babe's handle was jamming into my back.

"We're searching for an ancient stone," I said, trying to appear at ease despite the awkward angle of my body.

"Do I look as uncomfortable as she does?" Marjorie shifted on her stool. "I've told you a hundred times I need a chair with back support."

"When you become the crone, then you get the throne with back support," Miriam snapped.

Marjorie rolled her eyes. "Fat chance that'll ever happen. You've probably got vampire blood that makes you immortal."

"I'm a witch. If I had vampire blood then I'd be dead." Miriam returned her focus to the three of us. "Who's in charge?"

I held up a hand. "We're searching for an ancient artifact with summoning power that was part of Friseal's Temple."

Miriam frowned. "Friseal, you say? I thought it was a tower."

"I thought it was a ziggurat," Marjorie chimed in.

"See?" Kami whispered. "Not just us."

"Who's Friseal?" Meghan asked.

Miriam tried to snap her fingers but realized the black mitten was impeding her progress. She removed the mitten with her teeth and snapped her fingers. "Meghan, give her what she needs."

"Oh, right." Meghan slid off the stood and retrieved a pen and pad of paper from a hidden cabinet built into the cave wall. "Make your list, please."

"There's only one question," I told her.

"You still have to list it." Meghan thrust the items at me. I scribbled my 'list' and gave them back to her. She crossed the grotto and handed the pen and paper to Miriam.

"What do you think?" Kami asked.

"I think I'm looking at three witches and wondering why you need our help," Marjorie replied.

"Only one of us is a witch," Kami protested.

"Two of you are proper witches," Miriam said. She zigzagged the pen at me. "I don't know what's going on with you. You've got a strange energy I can't identify."

Briar laughed. "I'm not a witch either. I'm a shapeshifter."

Miriam rested her hands on the arms of the throne and leaned forward to peer at Briar. "Who told you that?"

Briar propped herself up on her elbows for a better view of the witches. "No one had to tell me. I shift."

"I shift, therefore, I am?" Miriam cackled. "It doesn't work that way, sweetie. Trust me, you're as much of a witch as that one." She flicked a finger at Kami.

"What do you shift into, hon?" Meghan asked. Her tone was gentler and kinder than the other two witches. I had a feeling if we came back in a few decades, Meghan would sound more like her companions. Life had a way of wearing down even the most patient people.

Briar winced. I knew how much she loathed this question.

"A beast," Kami answered for her. "A huge, terrifying beast."

"Does this beast have a name?" Marjorie asked.

"I just call her a beast, but I suppose I could give her a name." She cast a quizzical glance at me. "What's Grendel's mother's name from Beowulf?"

"Good goddess," Miriam said, exasperated. "Marjorie means what kind of animal do you shift into? A wolf?"

"Oh, no." Her gaze shifted to the floor. "Nobody knows. I'm just this huge, scary thing."

Miriam nodded, appearing satisfied. "See? I told you. Witch."

"How is that a witch?" Kami asked.

Miriam smoothed the white beard now resting on her lap. She looked like she was stroking a fluffy cat. "How do you know about Friseal, yet you don't grasp basic concepts about supernatural abilities? You inherited the ability to transform. That's your magic."

"But I only transform into a beast," Briar objected. "Shouldn't I be able to shift into anything I want?"

Miriam licked her lips and eyed Kami. "What's your power, sweetheart?"

"Mind control."

"You can't do telepathy?"

Kami shook her head.

"How about telekinesis?"

"No."

Miriam looked at Briar. "She has powers of the spirit, yet she can't perform more than one. So why should you expect to transform into more than one thing?"

"What about vampires?" Kami asked. "Some of them can transform into butterflies, but they're not witches. Otherwise, they'd be dhampirs like..." She paused and I noticed the muscle in her cheek pulse. "Like the offspring of vampires and other species."

"When Friseal's Temple was destroyed, powers merged and combined. There are traces of every species in all of us." Her gaze landed on me. "Some much more than others."

Interesting. "So you think vampires possess a form of magic?"

"The ones who can turn into butterflies do," Miriam said. "For whatever reason, that ability stuck and got passed down from generation to generation. That's my theory anyway. Others may disagree."

"Sort of makes the whole idea of vampire purism seem ridiculous," Briar said.

Miriam set the pen and paper on the arm of the throne. "I've always believed it was ridiculous anyway."

"What are your thoughts on chaos magic?" I asked.

Miriam looked at me with renewed interest. "I don't believe it exists as a separate category of magic. I believe it's as I just described. A mishmash of all magic that's been passed down from our ancestors. Prior to the temple..."

"Tower," Marjorie said.

"Ziggurat," Meghan chimed in.

"Prior to the structure built by Friseal and his followers, abilities were separate like the stones themselves. If you were an elemental witch, you possessed all the elemental abilities. Over time those abilities were diluted. Add on top of that the destruction of the stones and voila." She held out her hands, palms to the ceiling. "You have us."

Briar chewed her lip. "I'm a witch." She turned to face Kami. "All this time, I thought I wasn't one of you, but I am."

Kami slung an arm along her shoulders. "You were one of us regardless. We don't care which species you are. You're Briar Niall and you're a Knight of Boudica."

"This is all well and good," Miriam said, "but we have an appointment soon, so we really must get on with the show."

I gestured to the paper. "I gave you my question. We're ready."

Miriam clapped her hands once and they disappeared.

I looked beside me. Briar and Kami were gone, too.

I was alone in the grotto. The lights flickered and dimmed.

"Hello?"

"Who's there?" someone called back. I didn't recognize her voice.

"London."

"Ha! Good one. Are you supposed to be some sort of physical representation of the city we vanquished?"

I peered into the darkness of the grotto. "Who are you?"

A figure peeled away from the slick, shadowy wall of the cave. "Are you here to make me pay for my sins? Because, if so, I'm not interested."

She was a vampire, tall and statuesque. With her air of arrogance and striking features, I'd recognize her anywhere.

"Queen Britannia?"

She folded her arms and looked down her nose at me. "Who's asking?"

"I thought this was meant to be a vision," I said, more to myself. I shouldn't be able to interact with a vision.

"It is." She circled me slowly, eyeing me with a blend of curiosity and hunger. "And you are quite a vision."

I narrowed my eyes. What was happening?

"I'm searching for a stone and this vision is supposed to help me find it."

The queen extended her arms wide. "Feel free to search me. I haven't been touched by anyone in a long time. I wager I'd enjoy it."

I blinked. This was like a strange fever dream. I started to question whether I was even in Morpeth. Maybe I was still in the city with Yardley and something went wrong with the portal.

"You're dead."

She clucked her tongue. "How rude. I believe the expression you're looking for is 'otherwise engaged.'"

What did the queen have to do with the Summoning Stone? What kind of oracle was this?

"I think there's been a mistake."

"I hope not because I am famished." She ran her tongue over her top lip. "And you look scrumptious."

The vampire queen surged toward me and sank her fangs into my flesh. I released a blood-curdling scream and the grotto went black. When I opened my eyes again, I was still on the beanbag chair clutching my neck.

Briar kneeled beside me. "London, are you okay?"

It took me a second to adjust. "I think so."

"So?" Kami prompted. "Where's the stone?"

"I have no idea. It was a weird vision. It didn't make any sense."

"Our visions always make sense," Miriam protested. "One hundred percent guaranteed."

"Then I want my money back."

"You haven't paid," Miriam reminded me.

Briar appeared crestfallen. "We'll just keep looking then. This was only our first stop. For all we know, one of the other groups has already found it."

Kami snorted. "Fat chance. This stone has London's name written all over it. If anyone's going to find the stone, it's us."

I was glad someone had confidence in me because I wasn't feeling that optimistic.

"You can put your beard back on Santa. We're done here. This was a complete waste of time."

I struggled to get out of the beanbag and thrust my hand into the air for assistance. Briar tugged me to my feet.

"Don't be so dismissive. There's a reason you were brought to us," Marjorie said.

"Yeah, that reason is named Gwyneth," I shot back. "She probably trawls the gatehouse looking for suckers like us."

"Believe what you will, but I wouldn't be so quick to ignore what you learned here," Meghan said.

"I learned that I hate the smell of cloves," Kami told her. "So I guess this visit wasn't a total loss."

We exited the grotto. A few customers meandered around the shop, including a family of five. The three kids were grabbing items off the shelves with far too much exuberance for breakables.

"Who comes to Santa's Grotto so far from Christmas?" Briar whispered.

The mother must've overheard because she turned to face us. "People who need a reason to keep their kids going when the days are bleak and joyless." She inclined her head toward the youngest child—a boy around six. "He's on the tribute list. Hasn't been called yet, but made the list. Has nightmares about it now."

My gaze flicked to the grotto. I'd wondered why three witches would waste their talents in a place like this, but now I understood. Santa and her elves were similar to knights in that we each performed a public service. We used our abilities to ease the suffering of others. I felt a pang of guilt for my dismissal of the trio. If they believed there was something to learn in that vision, I was willing to believe it, too.

"I'm sorry," Briar said. "I didn't mean any disrespect."

The mother nodded and rejoined her family.

I turned toward the door and saw Kami sniffing a purplish-red candle.

"I had to get the smell of cloves out of my system." She held it toward me. "It's mulberry. Want to sniff?"

"No thanks. We should go."

"No beer?" She reluctantly returned the candle to the shelf. "Fine. No beer."

We left the shop and returned to clove-free air.

"Come see us again soon." Abby waved to us from the door. "We're here three-hundred sixty-four days a year."

Kami laughed. "I guess you have off for Christmas."

"No. New Year's Day," Abby said, and closed the door.

"Where to next?" Briar asked.

I gazed at the main thoroughfare. "No idea, but I doubt the stone is in Morpeth."

"What makes you so certain?" Kami asked.

"Because those three witches know about Friseal's Temple. I think they would've sensed it."

Kami cast me a sidelong glance. "You think their radar is that good?"

"It might not extend beyond the town border, but yes, I think it's that good."

Kami shoved her hands in her pockets. "Then I guess we're off to the next town."

"What's wrong with that?" Briar asked.

"It's cute here. I like the architecture. There's even a clock tower."

"You can always come back," I suggested. "Use some of those holidays you've accumulated that you never use."

"I guess." Kami flicked a glance at me. "What'd you see in the vision?"

I shook my head. "My head is filled with too many distractions. I think they got in the way of the message."

My phone buzzed in my pocket.

"Your butt's vibrating," Kami said.

"At least we know the satellites are working." I pulled out the phone, expecting to see the name of one of the knights. "Callan?"

"Hey, where are you?"

"Northumberland."

"Are you serious? How'd you get there so quickly?"

"Don't ask questions you don't want the answer to. We're tracking the stone. Your brother sent three teams to three counties and so have we."

"And where in this county are you?"

"Morpeth at the moment."

"Do you know where the gatehouse is?" he asked.

I frowned. "Yes."

"Wait there. I'm sending someone to you."

"Why? Do you know something? Did you speak to Maeron?"

"He seems to be hiding from me at the moment."

"Gee, can't imagine why."

"I know an excellent place for you to stay in Northumberland. You can't do a proper search if you're tired and hungry."

I relaxed. "You don't have to do that."

"I'll join you when I can."

"And you definitely don't have to do that." It was one thing for me to go up against Maeron. I didn't want to cause a battle between brothers.

"I beg your pardon, Miss Hayes. Are you trying to tell the Highland Reckoning what to do?"

"Wouldn't dream of it." I hung up the phone. "To the gatehouse, ladies. Looks like we're getting a royal welcome."

11

K ami, Briar, and I waited in front of the gatehouse and tried not to look conspicuous, which was kind of hard given our multitude of weapons. A black sedan pulled up to the curb and the driver's side window lowered.

"One of you is Miss Hayes, I presume." The driver looked about fifty albeit with a cherubic face and eyelashes that a doe would envy.

"Who wants to know?" I asked.

"My name is Morris. The prince asked me to collect you."

Kami aimed her crossbow. "Which prince determines whether I hit you with a bolt between the eyes."

Morris didn't flinch. "Callan, miss. Prince Callan. I'm the caretaker for Alnwick Castle. He said you might need somewhere to stay during your quest." He looked expectant. "You are knights, yes?"

Kami lowered her crossbow. "You're offering us rooms in a castle?"

Briar looked at me, wide-eyed. "When you said royal welcome, I thought you were exaggerating."

I shrugged. "So did I."

"I'm not sure we should stay somewhere that belongs to Prince Maeron," Kami said. "What if he turns up with his minions?"

Morris smiled, showing a set of surprisingly short fangs. "The castle belongs only to Prince Callan. It was a gift from King Casek on the prince's sixteenth birthday."

Kami shot me an aggrieved look. "I got a piece of bread with walnuts baked into it for my sixteenth birthday. That's the same, right?"

"You don't even like walnuts," I pointed out.

"I know. Don't you remember I had to spit them out? I felt like I was eating tiny brains." She cringed at the memory.

I heard the click of doors unlocking and Morris said, "There's ample room in the back for all three of you."

Kami cocked an eyebrow. "Do we trust this guy?"

I nodded. "I'm perfectly willing to believe that Callan owns his own castle that he's never mentioned."

Morris stepped out of the car to open the back door. "Would you like me to store your weapons in the boot?"

Kami hugged her crossbow. "No thanks. It's like my security blanket." She ducked into the car. "Although I won't object to a soft mattress and a fluffy pillow when we get there. Ooh, do you think there'll be one of those big bathtubs with the claw feet? I've always wanted to take a bubble bath in one of those."

Briar slid in beside her. "You do remember we're here to find an ancient stone that could unleash chaos on the world?"

"And I'd be much better equipped to do that after a luxurious soak in a tub."

"I'll sit with you in the front if you don't mind," I said.

He bowed slightly. "I would appreciate the company, Miss Hayes."

It took forty minutes to drive to Alnwick. I only realized we'd arrived when I noticed the silhouette of a sprawling castle ahead.

Kami stuck her head between the front seats for a better view. "It's huge."

"It dates from Norman times," Morris said. "Belonged to the Duke of Northumberland until the Eternal Night fell. Then it sat empty until it was gifted to the prince. He invested heavily in repairs."

"Why does it look familiar?" Briar asked.

"It was featured in many television shows and films before the Great Eruption," Morris explained.

"Cool."

"What's the nearest train station?" I asked. I wondered whether Maeron's Northumberland contingency would be posted nearby.

Morris pulled past a set of lion statues. "Alnmouth Station is about four miles from here. It used to run from Britannia City to Edinburgh, but now it terminates before the border."

"There's so much open space around here," Briar said. "Reminds me of my grandparents' home."

"There was a lovely garden at one time, but that disappeared after the Great Eruption. The prince had the option of hiring a magical staff to revive the garden, but he didn't want to use public funds for his own personal gain."

"Wouldn't everyone be able to enjoy it?" Briar asked.

Morris cast a glance at her over his shoulder. "Not without trespassing."

"He could open the whole castle to the public," Kami said. "Problem solved."

Morris pulled the car in front of the main entrance. "Imogen forbade it. She didn't want to set a precedent in case Prince Callan vacated the castle once he returned to the seat of House Duncan."

He stopped the car and opened the back door.

"I feel like we should have luggage," Kami said.

"Whatever you need, a member of staff will be happy to provide." Morris closed the car door and entered the castle.

Kami looped her arm through mine. "If not for the impending danger, this would feel like a holiday."

A vampire met us inside. She was average height with a slender build. Her curtain of reddish-brown hair and narrow eyes made her look like an angry Pekingese.

"This is Polly, the housekeeper," Morris said. "Now if you'll excuse me, I'll speak to the cook about a meal for our guests."

"Nice to meet you, Polly. I'm London. Prince Callan was kind enough to offer us accommodation during our visit to Northumberland."

Kami and Briar were too busy admiring their surroundings to introduce themselves.

"That staircase..." Kami said. "I've never seen anything like it."

The arched staircase seemed to go on forever, arriving at a gallery at the top.

"I feel like we're in a museum," Briar added.

I agreed. From the marble panels on the wall to the carvings on the ceiling, the castle didn't seem designed for defense. It seemed designed to showcase its architectural delights.

Polly scrutinized us. "Morris says you're knights on some kind of quest."

"Morris could stand to be a little more discreet," Kami said.

The housekeeper laughed. "I like you. What's your name?"

"Kamikaze Marwin."

"What kind of name is that?"

"What kind of name is Polly?" Kami shot back.

"You'd have to ask my mother, but that would require a talented seer and a seance." She gave Kami the once-over. "You don't look Japanese. Why'd your parents give you a Japanese name?"

"Do you know what Kamikaze means in Japanese?" Kami asked.

"Not particularly."

"It means divine wind."

Polly laughed. "So what? Your mother thought the gods delivered you to her on a cloud?"

"No, my mother had terrible gas throughout her pregnancy and was still holding a grudge at the time of my birth."

This time Polly threw her head back and laughed with abandon. "And what about you London? Let me guess. You were conceived in Britannia City, but your mother didn't want to name you after a vampire."

"I was and I'm sure she didn't, but she chose the name because she loved history."

Polly pretended to snore.

"My mother believed that once upon a time, London was one of the greatest cities in the world. She dreamed of a better future for me."

Polly grunted. "If she was going to be that sentimental, she could've just named you Hope."

I smiled. "That's my middle name."

Kami looked at me. "I didn't know that. How could I not know that?"

I shrugged. "I didn't know you were named after flatulence. Now we're even."

Briar raised her hand. "What about me?"

"What about you?" Kami asked.

Briar lowered her hand. "Doesn't anyone want to know about the origin of my name?"

"It means thorny shrub," Polly said. "It was also the name of Sleeping Beauty in some versions. I'm going to go out on a limb and say your mother was an avid reader of fairy tales."

Briar's mouth turned down at the corners. "So I guess my story isn't as interesting."

Polly's eyes turned to slits as she continued to focus on Briar. "You don't smell right."

Briar lifted her arms and sniffed. "I'm sure I could use a shower. We've been traveling..."

"I'm not talking about your sweat glands, missy. I'm talking about your very essence."

Briar gave me a sidelong glance that begged for help.

"Since when do vampires have a keen sense of smell?" Kami asked.

"Not all of us do, but I was blessed with one." Polly clasped her hands and offered a proud smile. "My mother would have me sniff out the food and drink that was about to go off so she could make sure to serve it next."

I thought about what I'd learned and wondered whether Polly had wolf blood somewhere in her family history.

Polly stepped closer and sniffed again, prompting Briar to take a step backward.

"You probably smell the beast within," Kami said.

Polly snorted. "There's no beast in this one."

"Trust me, there is. And you don't want to be there when it gets unleashed."

"She," Briar corrected her. "When *she* gets unleashed."

Polly angled her head, eyeing her with curiosity. "What kind of beast? You don't smell like a wolf to me. They usually have a damper scent."

Kami stifled a laugh. "Wet dog."

I placed a hand on Briar's shoulder. "She's our one-of-a-kind beast and she's very special."

Briar straightened her shoulders. "I'm a shapeshifter witch."

Polly gave us a crisp nod. "Very well then, shapeshifter witch. I'll show you to your quarters."

"Any chance there's a clawfoot tub somewhere in this castle?" Kami asked as we followed Polly up the grand staircase.

"You're in luck. We have one."

Kami turned to look at me with wide eyes. "First dibs."

"Fine, but don't take too long. Briar and I could both use a good soak too."

Our quarters were just as impressive as the rest of the rooms. My room included its own fireplace, a canopied bed, and portraits of solemn-looking people I'd never seen before. They appeared human rather than vampire and I wondered whether Callan had bothered to do much in the way of redecorating. Maybe not when he didn't seem to spend much time here.

Polly delivered towels and a bar of soap and Kami wasted no time rushing to the enjoy the many splendors the bathtub had to offer.

I took a nap until Briar woke me for my turn in the tub. As I undressed, I noticed a few flecks of silver on my arms. I sank into the water and released a bit of magic. The relaxing combination of bubbles and a magical release practically sent me into a coma. I dunked my head in the water and enjoyed the silence. It felt nice to clear my head. I sat up and flicked the bubbles off my hands. A knock at the door startled me.

"You already had your chance, Kami. Now it's my turn."

The door creaked open. "It isn't Kami."

I turned to see Callan's broad frame filling the doorway.

"I didn't mean to interrupt," he continued. "I only wanted to see you."

I leaned my chin on the edge of the tub. "You almost saw more than you bargained for."

"You wouldn't have had any complaints from me. Would you like me to leave? Now that I've seen you're alive and well, I'm happy to wait."

We stared at each other for a moment. I was completely naked and alone in a room with the Demon of House Duncan. I couldn't decide whether to be scandalized or overjoyed.

"Thank you for arranging this," I said.

He stepped into the room and closed the door. "I had nothing to do with your bubble bath, but I'm enjoying the scent...as well as the view."

"The scent is rosehip." I sat a little taller in the bath so that the curve of my breasts was visible above the water line. Pale pink bubbles clung to my skin.

"Doesn't smell floral. It's subtle." He drew closer and sniffed the air. "Smells woody."

"Because it isn't made from flowers."

"I like it."

He was now dangerously close to the tub.

I looked up at him. "Ever hear of personal space?"

His mouth twitched. "Is it wrong to be envious of bubbles?"

I scooted down so that my chin skimmed the surface of the water.

"You're going to end up with a bubble beard if you go any lower," he said.

"Why are you here, Callan?" I tried to inject a note of agitation into my voice, but I failed miserably. The truth was I was happy to see him—and from my current point of view, he was very happy to see me, too.

"I wanted to tell you that Maeron knows you're here. Apparently he has a spy."

I jolted upright and water spilled over the sides of the tub. "Here in the castle?"

"Seems likely. I'll be conducting a thorough..." His gaze flickered away from my face and I saw the desire in his eyes. "Very thorough examination."

I quickly folded my arms across my exposed chest. "Towel, please."

He inclined his head toward the table within reach of the tub. "It's folded right there."

"I know, but it would require me to move."

His smile broadened. "I know."

I narrowed my eyes at him. "You're supposed to be a gentleman, remember?"

He fluttered his eyelashes in mock innocence. "Am I? I don't recall anyone referring to me as the Gentleman of House Duncan."

I glared at him. "Smart ass. Is Maeron sending goons after me?"

"I warned him that if he did, he'd be forced to deal with me." He retrieved the towel and held it high enough that I'd have to rise out of the tub to reach it.

"Our leads are no better than his."

"No, but he still wants the other stones."

"Did you ask him to return the Immortality Stone?"

"Yes. Naturally he refused."

"Have you told the king? That might motivate him to act honorably."

"I opted to wait. My brother is misguided, but I promise you he isn't evil."

"You can promise all you like, but that's not been my experience." I held out my hand. "Now, either hand me the towel or I'll be forced to use magic to retrieve it, which we both know is illegal."

"Wouldn't want to bait you into breaking any laws." He dropped the towel and I caught it before it hit the water.

"If you don't mind, I'd like to finish in peace."

His gaze raked over my naked body, now somewhat visible beneath the layer of dissipating bubbles. "I wouldn't mind helping you...finish, but I know how much you prefer to complete tasks on your own." He winked and turned to leave.

My face grew hot. "A pleasure to see you again, Smart Ass of House Duncan!"

I tossed the towel onto the floor and submerged my head again to cool off.

ONCE THE KNIGHTS were clean and satiated, we left the castle to research possible locations of the stone.

"I think we should start with the fields," Briar said.

Kami stopped to tuck a dagger into her boot. "Why?"

"Because if the stone were in town, its influence would be more apparent. If it's buried somewhere in a field, the effects would be subtler."

She wasn't wrong. "Okay, you win. We'll start with open pastures."

"This isn't just an excuse to wander, is it?" Kami asked.

"No, absolutely not. Besides, London will know if we're on the right track. She has summoning powers, so she'll sense something. Isn't that right?"

I expelled a breath. "In theory, but who knows for certain?"

"Could it be in the river?" Kami asked.

I cast a glance in the direction of the River Aln. "It could be. It could also be in Cumbria or Durham."

Kami pursed her lips. "No idea. Got it."

"With the Spirit Stone, I felt a connection. Once I was within range, the energy guided me there. Hopefully that will happen again."

"Does that mean we have to work in silence?" Kami asked. "Because you know I'm not very good at that. Maybe we should ask your boyfriend if we can borrow a car. If we roll down the windows, you'd be able to sense something even at thirty miles an hour."

"Thirty miles an hour?" I scoffed. "Who's driving? Your grandma?"

"The car is a brilliant idea," Briar said. "We'll cover a lot more ground that way and be able to hide if we see Maeron's men. They'll never expect us to drive in a vampire-owned sedan."

"Fine." I marched back toward the castle entrance, but I was making the request of Morris not Callan. I hadn't seen the prince since our bath time rendezvous and I thought it best to keep it that way. He was a distraction I couldn't afford.

Once I secured the black sedan from Morris, we piled

into the car. As the most experienced driver among us, Briar took the wheel.

We rode through the countryside with the windows down, blasting music I didn't know the words to. I kept my senses at high alert. If the stone was here, I was determined to feel its energy.

As we approached another pasture, something pinged inside me. I felt like a metal detector.

"Stop here," I said.

Briar pulled the car off the road and parked. "You sense it?"

"I don't know what I sense yet but it's worth exploring."

We exited the car and locked the doors.

"Which way, Madam Radar?" Kami asked.

I pointed straight across the field. On Skye I felt energy pulses that guided me to the cove behind a waterfall where the stone was doubling as a giant's tooth. This felt different, but maybe it was because the magic was different.

We walked through the pasture. There was no sign of life. No sheep. No goats. Nothing. I didn't like it.

Briar's smile told me she was unfazed. "Look, it's a turnstile. I haven't seen one of these since I was kid visiting my grandparents. Let me show you how to get through..."

Kami vaulted straight over the fence and dusted off her hands. "Like that?"

"No." Briar maneuvered through the mechanical gate with a sour expression. "Like this."

I followed Briar's lead. No point in risking a splinter when there was a more civilized way to enter the adjacent field.

"Do you think there are cows?" Kami asked. "I would love to see one."

"A cow is on her bucket list," I told Briar. "I saw them in Devon, so I'm good."

Kami scowled. "Don't remind me. So unfair. If I'd gone with you, I would've been able to cross that one off."

"You also might've died," I pointed out. "Lots of danger on that trip."

"Yeah, but you seduced a vampire prince. Don't forget that part."

"I didn't seduce anyone. If anything, he tried to seduce me."

Briar frowned. "For a knight, I suddenly feel like I live a very sheltered life."

Kami cringed. "Holy hellfire. What's that smell?"

I inhaled. The air reeked of manure.

"Today might be your lucky day," I said.

There were no lights in the area so we ventured carefully. One wrong step and we'd have a twisted ankle on our hands.

"I didn't realize animals could smell this bad," Kami said.

I cut her a sidelong glance. "You thought they pooped rainbows and flowers?"

Kami's hand shot out to grasp mine. "Gods above, I can't believe it."

"What?"

She pointed ahead. I followed her finger to the middle of the field where a solitary figure chewed on grass. Its brown coat was barely visible in the gloaming, but the silhouette was plain as day.

Kami turned to me and smiled. "Let's moo-ve." Quickening her pace, she started toward the cow. She managed to get within two feet of the creature when I heard a click.

"Step away from the cow and raise your hands in the air," a voice ordered.

Slowly I pivoted to see a gray-haired woman in glasses leveling a shotgun at us. She couldn't have been taller than five feet.

I held up my hands. "We're not here for the cow, I promise."

She eyed us over the barrel. "You're not ogres or demons. What are you?"

Kami kept her hands in the air. "Knights."

The woman chuckled, maintaining her grip on the shotgun. "You don't look like any knights I've ever seen."

"And how many have you seen?" Kami challenged.

"Is that why you're loaded down with all those weapons?"

"Yes, we're on a quest," Briar said.

"Is that so? You help people in need—stuff like that?"

"Generally speaking," I replied.

"For money," Kami added.

I kicked her in the side of the ankle. Now was not the time to be greedy.

"In that case, will you help us?"

"Hard to say no when you've got a gun aimed at us," I said.

The woman lowered the shotgun. "We have so little as it is and we've been terrorized by ogres for months. They eat our livestock and ransack our supplies. Thankfully they haven't managed to devour our cows yet. We always have someone watching them when they're eating. That's why I'm here now."

Kami blew a relieved breath. "We'll help you."

I shot her a quick look. "Later. Right now we're committed to another task."

Kami pulled a face. "Are you not listening? Cows are at stake, London."

The odd energy I'd sensed intensified.

"Ogre alert," Briar said.

The old woman lifted her shotgun. "Point me in the right direction."

I saw a round-shouldered figure lumbering up the hill to our left. Two more followed close behind.

Three ogres.

They looked like a row of Russian nesting dolls with each ogre being a smaller version of the one next to it.

"Goody. A friend for each of us." Kami unhooked a lasso that had been attached to her hip. "Lady, you might want to take a few steps back and save your ammo for another day."

I looked at Kami. "What are you going to do? Round them up?"

Kami patted the lasso. "Minka enchanted this rope for me before we left."

Two more ogres climbed into view. Unfortunately at eight and seven feet tall, respectively, they were even larger versions of the others.

"They could at least have the decency to arrive in order," Kami complained. She twirled the lasso in the air and yipped like a cowgirl from the American Old West.

Briar and I traded looks.

I shrugged. "I guess we're going on the offensive."

"I would've preferred to wait until they actually did something before attacking them," Briar said.

Kami continued to twirl the lasso. "Why do you think I'm using the rope and not the crossbow?"

"They're here for the cow," the old woman shouted. "If you wait until they do something, we'll lose Bessie too."

Kami's eyes rounded. "They can't lose Bessie."

Briar produced a gun.

"Where did you get that?" I demanded.

"Don't worry." She aimed and fired at the largest ogre. "Tranquilizer darts."

The ogre's skin was thicker than it looked. The dart bounced off and landed on the ground. The ogre stared at it, his wide face contorted with confusion. He lifted his gaze and noticed the gun in Briar's hand.

Oops.

Offense quickly became defense as the ogres charged.

"They're faster than they look," Kami said, tossing the loop around the middle ogre and tugging. "You'd think all that bulk would slow them down."

I was curious to see what the enchanted rope did to the ogre, but I was too busy fending off the second largest ogre who seemed to have decided I'd make a nice hood ornament for his car. He lifted me by the waist and slammed me onto the ground. I accessed my magic and created a cushion of air between my feet and the ground to soften the landing.

Out of the corner of my eye, I saw Briar fire off darts at the two smaller ogres. They staggered into each other like two drunk old men on their way home from the pub after last call.

The ogre that attacked me came back for seconds.

"Two can play at this game," I murmured.

I connected to my magic and peeled off another version of myself.

"What in the hell?" the old woman yelled. "What kind of magic is that?"

Briar stopped shooting to gaze at me. "I think I got hit on the head. I'm seeing double."

Kami looked at my carbon copy. "No. You're seeing one of London's powers."

I conjured another version of myself to help the first one take down the second largest ogre. That left the real me to handle the largest one.

"They're not very susceptible to mind control," Kami said. "I don't think their brains are developed enough."

That usually made it easier for me when it came to animals. I could commandeer the hell out of a goldfish.

The ground shook.

Kami stared at the field beneath her feet. "Earthquake?"

Not an earthquake. Footsteps.

It seemed there was one more ogre bringing up the rear and he was a doozy.

By the time the big guy crested the hill, I was ready for him. All three of me were. We used elemental magic in tandem to immobilize him, pushing the air into him from three sides. Once he was trapped in our wind triangle, Kami looped the neck over his head—at least she tried to.

"His head's too big," she said. "I need to loosen the knot and widen the loop."

I remained focused on controlling the air. "Briar, can you try the gun?"

"I'm out of darts, not that they'd work on him anyway."

Kami struggled with the knot. "Fine motor skills are not my strong suit."

The ogre strained against the air magic and I could feel myself losing my grip.

"Hurry, Kami!"

The ogre's foot shot out and he kicked Kami across the ground. She rolled across the field and landed next to the cow.

The big ogre turned his attention to me. Uh oh.

"This has all been a misunderstanding," I said.

He grunted.

"My friend wasn't trying to kill you."

He lumbered forward and swiped left. I dodged his hand and danced out of reach.

"Should I unleash the beast?" Briar called.

"No." Briar's monster form guaranteed extreme violence and I was still trying to avoid any permanent injuries.

The ogre's nostrils flared. Even worse, his cohorts were starting to regain consciousness. I was beginning to regret following my instincts.

The old woman leveled her shotgun. "The whole village will starve if they keep coming back."

Kami jogged over to rejoin us. "Can't you send them somewhere special if you know what I mean?"

"No, I can't." The second the words left my mouth, an idea took shape. "But I have another plan."

The fallen ogres began to rise.

Briar nudged me. "Whatever it is, hurry. I'm out of darts."

I shifted gears and connected to my earth magic. Suddenly the smell of dirt and grass seemed more potent.

Kami aimed her crossbow. "Come on, London."

I spent so much time downplaying my abilities, I never tried to use the full extent of them. Now seemed like a good time to experiment.

"Get behind me," I barked.

The ogres raced forward. I whipped Babe over my head and brought the axe down hard. The earth yawned. The ogres stumbled and collapsed into each other. I concentrated on the gap and *pulled*.

The earth opened wide enough to swallow them whole.

Kami leaned forward and peered into the pit. "Oh, look. Timmies fell down the well."

I maintained my focus and *pushed*. The ground groaned

as it shifted. I didn't close the gap all the way, only enough to trap the ogres without suffocating them.

It felt good to use that much magic. It felt right.

"Could be worse, fellas," Kami called to them. "Could be Tartarus."

I released my hold on the earth and looked at the old woman. "They won't be breaking free anytime soon. How you handle them is up to you."

The old woman stared into the abyss. "Hell if I know. I'll have to call an emergency meeting with the town council. Maybe we'll let the vampire authority deal with it. Make use of those tax dollars."

"You're welcome," Kami said.

The three of us marched past the chasm and headed back to the car.

Kami cast a last glance at the cow. "What do you call a cow after an earthquake?"

I smacked my face. "Don't."

She turned her grin to Briar. "A milkshake."

12

I spent the remainder of the day with my head stuck out of the car window trying to sense any energy pulses.

"I think you missed your true calling as a canine companion," Kami said from the back seat.

"And you missed yours as a standup comedian," I shot back.

Hours later we returned to Alnwick Castle, hungry and no more knowledgeable about the location of the stone. I was disappointed to learn that Callan had left not long after us and had yet to return. Neither Polly nor Morris knew his whereabouts.

"I don't think you fully grasp my role here," Polly said, after I'd fired off a dozen questions regarding Callan's disappearance. "I'm not his nan. He's my employer."

"London wants to know whether to request an extra blanket tonight or whether her boyfriend will be here to keep her warm." Kami bit into a gravy-stained roll that Polly had provided.

We sat a table in the kitchen where the cook had prepared a root vegetable stew in anticipation of our return.

Polly had tried to persuade us to eat in the formal banquet hall, but we insisted on the kitchen. Less fuss.

Polly remained standing. She apparently drew the line at joining guests at the table. "Tell me more about this quest of yours. Are there dragons involved? I know they can be a nuisance, but I happen to like dragons."

I speared a carrot. "So do I."

Polly got a faraway look in her eye. "When I was a girl, I used to spend hours down at Bolam Lake trying to befriend dragons. I'd even hide food from dinner in my skirts so I had a treat to offer them later."

I smiled. "That sounds nice."

Polly's mouth formed a thin line. "Not always. I had to be careful and always take a weapon with me."

Briar stopped mid-chew. "Some of the dragons attacked you?"

"Not unless there was a nest, but I knew to avoid them. No, it was the other monsters I worried about. That lake attracts as many dangerous creatures as it does dragons, you see. My gran used to say it was the water. There's some kind of chemical imbalance that draws the monsters."

I set down my fork. "Can you define the word 'monsters?'"

"Strange ones," Polly said. "They seemed different from the usual monsters that came with the Great Eruption. It's one of the reasons we finally moved away. I got attacked by a hawk with a human head. Had nightmares for a year. It was the final straw for my family."

"Can you describe some of the other monsters?" I asked.

Polly shuddered. "Ooh, now, you're making me relive some unpleasant memories. Multiple heads, arms, legs— you name it and one of those creatures had it."

"Did anyone report the problems to House Lewis?" I asked.

She looked at me blankly. "Why would we do that?"

"You're vampires living in their territory. Why wouldn't you?"

Polly grunted. "No offense to His Highness, he's a lovely lad, but House Lewis doesn't pay much attention to what goes on between the capital city and Hadrian's Wall. There's nothing very glamorous about these parts."

"Where's Bolam Lake?"

"About thirty miles south of here."

"Uh oh. I recognize that look, London," Kami said.

Briar scrunched her nose. "You want to fight monsters now? Shouldn't we be searching for the stone."

"We're searching for the Summoning Stone," I reminded her. "Could be that the lake doesn't attract monsters. It produces them."

Briar's eyes widened. "The stone is somewhere at the bottom of the lake?"

"It's possible." It would explain the monster infestation. The stone summoned creatures residing on other planes and they emerged from the lake and into this world. Some of them might return the way they came. Others might stay and terrorize local communities or die trying.

"We need Stevie," Briar said. "I'm no good to you in a lake."

Kami looked at her. "You can swim, can't you?"

"Of course, but Stevie's our water witch."

"We don't have time to wait for Stevie. It isn't like Yardley can teleport her to us." Kami aimed her fork at me. "Besides, we've got our own water witch."

Briar licked a spot of gravy from the corner of her mouth. "You're sure you can handle it?"

"I'm not sure of anything, but we have to try. If Maeron gets there first..." I couldn't bring myself to finish the sentence. The Summoning Stone in the wrong hands could be catastrophic. Just because Callan believed his brother wasn't evil didn't mean he wasn't dangerous.

Kami slumped against the back of her chair. "I take it that means we're not sleeping tonight."

I pushed back my chair. "Rest is overrated."

Briar leaned her cheek against the palm of her hand. "Maybe for you. Some of us aren't fueled by magical energy."

"Oh, that reminds me. Morris has refilled the tank for you," Polly said.

"See? It's kismet." I stood and stretched my arms over my head. "When Callan gets back, will you please tell him where we've gone? But no one else. Not a soul."

Polly pretended to lock her lips.

Kami hurriedly scraped the last of the stew into her mouth before standing. "If I'm going to have a final meal, that was a pretty good one."

Polly smirked. "I'll be sure to give your regards to the cook."

Briar reluctantly rose to her feet. "Could I at least use the loo first?"

"Me first." Kami raced from the kitchen with Briar right behind her.

"Good luck," Polly said. "I'd love to be able to return to the lake someday without worry."

And I'd love to return to the city without worry. If we succeeded, then maybe we'd both get what we wanted.

.   .   .

THE DRIVE to Bolam Lake was uneventful. I offered to drive to let the others nap in the back, but they weren't keen.

"I've seen you drive," Kami said.

I gave her a pointed look. "Callan let me drive."

"Because it was part of his mating ritual. I slept with you for years. I don't have that incentive."

"You slept next to me," I corrected her.

"Whatever." Kami slid behind the wheel. "I'm awake enough. You roll down your window and focus on the stone."

Briar yawned. "Good. More room for me to stretch out in the back."

We left Alnwick and headed south.

Kami peered through the glass. "It's so much darker here than the city. I don't know how people live around here. Why don't they demand more lights?"

"You heard Polly. This is a forgotten area."

"A neglected one, more like. You'd think Callan would say something to the king."

"He probably doesn't notice. I don't think he spends much time here. Besides, he's a vampire. Darkness is second nature to him."

"And everybody else is too terrified to complain. Sounds about right." She looked at me sideways. "Maybe you could mention this to your new family?"

I laughed. "The king doesn't know who I am." And even if he did, I was hardly in a position to negotiate. I'd be lucky if he let me live.

A strange, guttural noise drew my attention to the back seat. "I didn't know Briar snored."

"Like the beast inside her."

"It's not inside her, remember? It's just the form her magic takes."

Kami grunted. "Weird, right? There's so much about the world we don't understand."

"I think it's always been that way. Before the Great Eruption, I bet humans thought they understood far more than they actually did."

"Well, they paid the price for their ignorance, that's for sure."

"And we're much the same."

Kami's gaze flicked to me. "Yeah, I guess we are."

My body began to hum. It was low and sporadic at first, but grew stronger as we passed the sign for Bolam Lake. I was both relieved and terrified.

"I think the stone might be here."

Kami tightened her grip on the wheel. "You don't sound very certain."

"I feel something familiar." I closed my eyes and tried to pinpoint the source of the energy pulses.

"Why can't I feel it?" Kami asked.

"Probably because you don't have any summoning magic in your genes. I bet you would've felt the Spirit Stone."

Briar poked her head between the seats. "Are we there yet?"

"Yes," I said.

"And so is the stone," Kami added.

"Maybe. Let's not get our hopes up."

Kami parked the car. We vacated the car and strapped on our weapons.

It was too dark to see the lake, but I sensed the water. The closer we got, the more certain I became about the stone. The water and the stone were two distinct sensations. The lake was a smooth hum in the background, whereas the stone's signal was acute and insistent.

Kami approached the edge of the lake. "Where are all the monsters? I thought we'd be fighting our way through them."

I adjusted the position of my daggers. "Don't sound so disappointed."

"You won't find many monsters here anymore," a voice said.

We turned to see a white-bearded man in a tweed jacket and tan trousers holding a walking stick. A border collie stood beside him panting and wagging his tail.

"Do you mind if I pet your dog?" Doomsday scenario or not, I couldn't resist a friendly canine.

"His name's Chutney."

Chutney immediately licked my proffered hand.

"What happened to the monsters?" I asked, rubbing the dog behind the ears.

"A group of us got together and asked the local vampire authority to have a ward installed. One of our neighbors lost a set of twins to a creature from the deep and there was outrage." He eyed the water with an expression bordering on resentment. "We raised half the funds ourselves and convinced the authority to pay the other half. Wards like that don't come cheap."

Too bad that didn't happen before Polly's family moved.

"What does the ward do?" I asked.

"You'd have to ask the wizards who created it. All I know is the monsters come less frequently than before. Some of the stronger ones manage to break through every now and again, but it's much better than it was."

I turned to gaze at the water. The lake's flat surface resembled a dark mirror. "Do people swim in it now that it's warded?"

"They do when there's an organized event with safety

measures in place. Lights get set up and there are lifeguards. I don't recommend swimming here alone."

"Be that as it may, we're going to take a swim in the lake," I told him. "You and Chutney might not want to stick around in case we attract unwanted visitors."

The man tugged his beard. "Why do I get the feeling you ladies aren't here for a picnic?"

"We're knights from Britannia City," Kami said.

"Is that so? What are you doing this far north? We don't get many visitors from the capital."

"We're looking for a magical artifact and we have reason to believe it's in this lake," I said. "If we find it, it might solve your monster problem."

His brow lifted. "That's good news. Chutney and I will get out of your way and let you work." He ambled away with Chutney at his heels, using his stick for support.

Briar watched them go. "I miss Trio."

I missed Trio and the menagerie, too, but now wasn't the time to commiserate. I kicked off my boots.

"Let's divide and conquer. Kami, you take the left. Briar, take the right." I'd handle the murky middle.

I swam to the center of the lake and then headed to the bottom. The water was relatively clear, probably because the lake was man-made. According to Polly, the lake had been created in 1972 as a recreational area.

As far as bodies of water went, this one wasn't particularly large—the circumference was about a mile—but there was still a lot of ground for only three of us to cover. I focused on the tugging sensation and tried to let it guide me to the stone.

After what seemed like hours of swimming, Kami appeared ahead of me and gestured to the top. I kicked my legs and we broke the surface at the same time.

"Did you find it?" I asked.

"I found a fossil. That's cool, right?"

"A fossil?"

"Looks like a shell."

"Describe the design."

Her head bobbed in the water. "What's there to describe? It's a spiral. A whorl like the pads of our fingers." She wiggled her fingertips.

"An ammonite?"

"How should I know? You're the educated one."

I flipped through my memories from the Atheneum. I had to have seen the marking for this stone, even if I hadn't been fully aware of it at the time. I strained to remember bur couldn't.

Another fact pushed its way to the front, one that rendered the marking moot.

"I think you found it," I said.

Kami brightened. "I did?"

Hope beat in my chest. "I think so. This lake is man-made."

Understanding glimmered. "There shouldn't be any ammonites."

"Show me."

She slipped beneath the surface and I followed. Briar must've noticed our discussion because she appeared beside me as we swam deeper.

The energy pulses grew stronger.

We reached the bottom and Kami pointed.

This one, a voice whispered in my head.

Come to mama.

Kami tried her best to dislodge it, but the stone was entrenched in the earth. Briar waved her aside and made an attempt. The stone shifted slightly.

The ground trembled.

I debated letting Briar try to rip it out in her beast form, but her paws would be too massive to work the edges of the stone.

Every minute we lost was a minute that could allow Maeron's team to catch up to us.

I waved them aside. I didn't waste time on brute strength. I had many advantages, but that wasn't one of them. I concentrated on the ground surrounding the stone and used my magic to *push*.

Kami and Briar retreated to the surface for air while I kept working on the stone. My elemental magic was coming into its own now. Water around me, earth to move, air in my lungs. All I needed was metal and fire and it was a party.

The stone shifted again. A small but significant movement. I continued to manipulate the ground around it.

I felt a surge of power as the earth expelled the stone. It floated just above the lake bottom. I swiped the stone and propelled myself to the surface. I was all smiles until I saw the expression on my companions' faces. I followed their troubled gazes to the water's edge, where a cluster of monsters awaited us. The removal of the stone seemed to have broken the ward, or at least weakened it.

I glared at the stone. "You could've at least had the decency to give us a thirty-second head start."

The stone stared back at me, silent.

"What's the plan?" Kami asked. "We can't tread water forever."

Briar shot her a quizzical look. "What makes you think they can't swim?"

Kami pressed her lips together. "My sunny optimism?"

"Look on the bright side," I said. "No kelpies." They were basically aquatic rats, ubiquitous except larger and deadlier.

The creatures blocked our path to the car. We'd have to circumvent them or cut straight through them. We swam away from the monsters toward a different shoreline.

The monsters seemed to lose sight of us as we exited the lake.

"I'll go first and clear a path," Briar said. "You two head for the car with the stone."

"What about my shoes?" Kami asked. "My favorite boots are over there."

I shook my head. "There will be other boots."

"Not like those," she grumbled.

Briar streaked ahead. She sprouted fur and exploded into her own monster form that towered over the creatures.

Kami prepared her crossbow.

I was so intent on the monsters ahead, I almost failed to notice the demons next to us, climbing out of the ground like moles. They looked like moles, too, with coarse, brown fur and beady eyes. Make that a dozen beady eyes each. Ew.

I unsheathed Babe and replaced it with the stone. I slung the axe over my shoulder and faced the demons. "Bad news, friends. I'm the whack-a-mole champion of Britannia City." Or at least I would be if that were a real competition.

I launched myself at them, swinging my axe with precision that would've impressed me if I'd had time to pause for contemplation. With every whack, demon goop splattered onto my armor and I hoped it didn't contain any deadly chemicals.

"No fair," Kami called over her shoulder. "Your game looks more fun."

I glanced over to see her fighting a monster that looked like a white, winged Yeti. Where had that guy come from?

Once I whacked the final demon, I scanned the area for more monsters. My skin was itching like crazy. There had to be more. Briar towered over a pile of bodies with blood dripping from her jowls. Even from this distance, her sharp fangs gleamed. Kami's winged Yeti was facedown on the ground, unmoving.

Something felt off.

"Get to the car," I yelled.

Kami raced to retrieve her boots and tossed me mine. I managed to slip on the second boot as a shriek pierced the air. Out of the darkness, a human-faced hawk swooped toward me. I sent my axe sailing through the air. The monster tried to jerk to the side at the last second. The blade sliced off a wing and sent the creature spiraling to the ground.

I ran to retrieve Babe just as another monster made its entrance. Holy hellfire. She was seven feet tall and naked from the waist up. Six arms, four legs, green skin, and snakes for hair. Despite the perky boobs, she wasn't winning any beauty pageants in this realm.

"You should've gone for a third nipple," I said. "Some people are into that sort of thing."

A dart shot out from the left boob and narrowly missed the top of my shoulder. What the hell?

The dart nailed the creature lurking behind me. The small alligator-type demon keeled over and died on the spot.

Shit. Poisonous boobs?

I spun back to my new opponent and shifted to magic. There were too many appendages. One axe wouldn't be enough.

My body was humming with magical energy. The stone seemed to have unlocked more of my potential and my system was in danger of overheating. I noticed the silver that dotted my skin. Well, at least I had an outlet.

Dust kicked up around us. Coughing, I closed my eyes and turned away. When I turned back around, the snake lady was gone.

My gaze swept the area but there was no sign of her.

Kami ran over, almost out of breath. "Where'd she go?"

"I don't know. I think I might've sent her somewhere by accident." Although I couldn't typically open portals without a ritual, the presence of the Summoning Stone meant all bets were off. Fingers crossed I didn't send her to the holiday home though. Unlike me, the snake lady had a hand for each stone hidden there.

A one-eyed creature emerged from the lake. The cyclops didn't seem too tall—until I realized he wasn't treading water but standing at the bottom of the lake.

"I've got the pirate," Kami yelled.

"Pirate?" I queried as she ran past me.

She positioned herself at the water's edge and raised the crossbow. "He's wearing a patch, isn't he?"

"No. Just aim for the eye you can see." I turned around to check on Briar. She was in beast form, tearing the limbs off another multi-armed creature.

My fingers curled around the handle of the axe. "Whatever we do, we have to protect the stone from them."

Kami aimed her crossbow and let another bolt fly. "How? There are only three of us and more keep coming."

She was right. It had been a mistake for us to separate into three groups to search for the stone. We thought we were saving time by covering more ground, but we'd divided our strength and now they would conquer.

A loud boom brought my hands to cover my ears. I looked up to see an iron cauldron whizzing across the sky like a witchy UFO. A white-haired woman climbed onto the lip of the cauldron. She wore a cloak tipped with skulls. My chest tightened.

It was Bertha, the thunder witch.

When I was eight, my mother told me a story about a supernatural hag named Bertha who ate her victims. The description had been too upsetting for me and I'd asked her to never tell me that story again. My mother had smiled and told me not to worry, that unlike the monsters that emerged during the Great Eruption, Bertha was a myth.

Thanks for shattering that belief, Summoning Stone.

Bertha jumped from the edge of the cauldron and landed about eight feet in front of me with surprising grace. The skulls on her cloak crashed into each other.

I gestured to the cloak. "Gives new meaning to a threat to bang heads together."

Bertha didn't crack a smile. "I don't know where I am or why you've summoned me, but I can tell you right now, I'm none too pleased about it. I was in the middle of a very tasty meal. It's never the same once you have to reheat."

"I didn't summon you. No one did."

She eyed me suspiciously. "Who are you?"

"Someone who doesn't want to fight you. Go back from where you came and I won't have to hurt you."

The witch cackled. "I love a woman with confidence."

She thrust out her hands and the skulls flew forward, abandoning the cloak. They elongated into full-sized skeletons and their eye sockets burned with white-hot fire.

Okay, *that* was not in the story my mother told me.

I connected to my magic. If I could use my transcendence ability to create more versions of myself, we'd have a fighting chance.

The skeletons lunged at the same time.

I slashed and punched, unable to peel off a layer. Out of

the corner of my eye, I saw a dozen more mole demons popping out of the ground.

There wasn't time for more complicated magic. I called upon the most easily accessible magic and let it fly. Gusts of wind. Shaking the earth. I couldn't pause long enough to make a coherent plan. I was stuck on defense.

Another winged Yeti buzzed past me and tackled Kami to the ground. I couldn't see Briar anymore.

I debated letting myself go nuclear like I did with the werewolves on Romeo's rooftop, but I couldn't control that power. I risked taking out my friends along with the monsters.

The skeletons were too numerous. I was trapped in a tower of bones. They ripped off my sheath and the stone tumbled out. Every bone my axe chopped, the skeletons were able to quickly reassemble. I could no longer see Bertha or hear her cackle and I worried for my friends.

A hard object slammed into the back of my skull and blood filled my mouth. Another one crashed into the bridge of my nose. The skeletons were using their own parts as weapons. Every time I connected to my magic, another jolt of pain cut me off again.

I fell to the ground and they climbed on top of me like scavengers ready to pick the meat from my limbs. I kicked and clawed the ground. Pain radiated from more places than I could count. I saw the stone just out of arm's reach. I twisted and my foot shot out to try to capture it. Instead I kicked it away. The stone rolled.

The skeletons disappeared.

I peered around me. There was no sign of any monsters. No Bertha. Kami was on the ground a few feet away, face-down. Soft groans reached my ears. She was alive.

As much as I wanted to breathe a sigh of relief, I couldn't

—and not only because my ribs were too sore. Every hair on my body was standing on end. Despite the monsters' disappearance, the danger hadn't passed.

I rolled to the side and winced from the pain. A line of silhouettes advanced toward us.

Make that two lines.

Kami raised her chin from the ground. "Cavalry?"

Even before I saw their familiar banner, I knew. "No," I croaked.

These vampires and wizards belonged to House Duncan.

King Glendon had discovered the location of the stone —whether through Maeron or another method, I wasn't sure. Not that it mattered. His team was here now, in House Lewis territory.

I crawled on my stomach toward the stone. Even my expensive magical armor wasn't enough to defend against the many hits I'd taken. I became aware of a wet spot on my hip and realized the dark blue fabric had been replaced by a patch of blood. I'd worry about the damage later. Right now I had to get that stone.

Heavy boots thudded toward me. I was inches away from the stone. My hand shot out and a boot came down hard on my arm. Bone crunched and I cried out. A hand reached down and picked up the stone.

"His Majesty thanks you for your service," a voice said.

There would be no witty comeback. Pain paralyzed me. I remained on the ground with a throbbing head and broken bones. I heard a cry of agony and realized it was coming from me.

Kami dragged herself over to me on her hands and knees. Her face was smeared with blood. I couldn't tell whether it was hers or someone else's.

"Briar?" I croaked.

"Still breathing."

That wasn't an encouraging response.

"They took the stone," Kami whispered.

"I know."

That simple statement stole the last of my reserves. I closed my eyes and succumbed to the pain.

13

I walked through a meadow and smelled the mixture of grass and flowers. All around me the sky was painted with the muted colors of sunrise. Although my brain recognized the impossibility, my body moved forward, as though this was the most natural thing in the world.

A figure stood at the edge of the meadow facing away from me. Her hair hung loose down her back and flecks of brilliant light filtered through her that made her appear pixelated.

Mother?

Soft petals brushed my ankles as I approached the figure. The closer I got, the wider my smile grew.

Finally she turned and my smile dissipated. Although I recognized the woman, she wasn't my mother. I'd never met her; I'd only seen her image carved from marble and painted on canvas.

And, more recently, in a vision.

Queen Britannia.

Her gaze raked over me with the kind of condescension I

would expect from the vampire queen. She seemed to find me lacking because her lip curled.

Right back at you, you raging narcissist.

"You expected someone else," she said, more of a statement than a question. The queen struck me as someone who only made statements. Questions were beneath her.

"I thought you were my mother."

"Ah. Then at least you're not here to kill me. Is she on another plane of existence?"

"She's dead."

The queen's hard expression didn't waver. "I see."

"What is this place?" And why was I dreaming about Britannia? Why not my mother?

She spread her arms wide. "Welcome to my hellscape, darling."

"I don't understand."

"Clearly." She cocked her head and examined me. "You're a witch."

Even in a dream, I was afraid to reveal the truth about myself to a vampire. "Yes."

She sighed. "I suppose you'll have to do."

"Do what?"

She ignored me. "It would help to know a little bit more about you. We'll need to utilize your strengths." Her gaze flickered over me. "Assuming you have any."

"I have enough."

Her eyes sparked with interest. "Tell me this much—is that bastard Glendon dead yet?"

"No, but I wish he were."

"Then we're on the same page. An excellent start. The first thing I intend to do upon my return is rip off his..." She stopped and looked at me. "How did you get here?"

"I'm not here." This was a dream, not reality. I pinched my arm. "Wake up, London."

"You're very much awake and I'm very much alive. I would appreciate it if you could get me out of here. I have lands to conquer and scores to settle."

The earth trembled beneath my feet.

In the distance, someone called my name.

The queen stared at the ground with resentment. "No fair."

A chasm opened beneath my feet and swallowed me whole. I heard a sharp intake of breath and clutched my chest.

It was me.

I opened my eyes and adjusted to the darkness. There was no meadow. No sunrise. No queen. I was in a bedroom. I glanced at the silky white sheets.

Alnwick Castle.

I drew myself to a seated position as the door cracked open. Kami's head poked through the doorway. She brightened when she saw me.

"You're awake." She leaned back and yelled. "She's awake!"

Kami burst into the room, quickly followed by Briar and the rest of the Knights of Boudica. They crowded around my bed, prompting me to pull up the sheets.

"I feel like a bug under a microscope."

"You were splat like one, too," Kami said. "Good thing Callan found the local healer."

"Callan?" I murmured.

"He found us," Briar said. "Polly told him where we went and he came to help."

"Sounds like he was a little late to the party," Neera said.

Briar patted my leg under the sheet. "I'm so relieved you're awake. We've been worried."

"How long have I been out?"

Kami pressed her lips together, as though uncertain how to answer. "Two days."

Two days. No wonder the rest of the team had arrived. They'd had ample time to get here.

"I had the strangest dream."

"If it involves a scarecrow and a tin man, that's already a book and a movie," Kami said.

I shook my head. "I was in a sunny meadow."

"Sounds like heaven to me," Neera said.

"I thought it was a dream about my mother. There was a woman there with me."

"Was she an angel?" Briar asked.

I laughed. "Far from it. She was a vampire."

"Well, that sucks. Or bites." Kami scratched her cheek. "What happened in the dream?"

I tried to remember the specifics. "It was Queen Britannia. She seemed annoyed."

Kami snorted. "Sounds about right."

Stevie gave my hand a gentle squeeze. "Doesn't surprise me. The last thing you saw was a bunch of vampires."

The realization of that moment hit me and I bolted upright. "Glendon has the Summoning Stone."

Kami's mouth curved downward. "They know, London."

"Is it such a big deal?" Ione asked. "If you have three of them and Maeron has one, we're still in the lead."

"It's not about being in the lead," I explained. "These stones are powerful weapons." I surveyed the inquisitive faces in the room. I needed them to understand the importance of recovering the stones. "Maeron has taken the Immortality, too. We need both."

"But House Lewis has had possession of the Immortality Stone for centuries," Neera pointed out. "Does it matter if they keep that one?"

"What will you even do when you get the other two stones?" Stevie asked.

Ione crossed her arms. "If they're so dangerous, we should destroy them."

Briar frowned. "Is that even possible?"

"I don't know." I'd been so focused on finding them, I hadn't thought of what to do with them. "I would think so, since the rest of them were destroyed.

"By gods," Neera emphasized. "Not by a ragtag group of knights."

Ione leaned a knee on the edge of the bed. "But destroying the stones won't eliminate the abilities connected to them, right? Vampires aren't going to stop being immortal because you destroyed the Immortality Stone."

I accepted the glass of water Stevie offered to me and took a sip. "No, but it will keep any single party from using them to control other species. Think about it. With Glendon in control of the Summoning Stone, he can wreak havoc on witches and wizards with that power, *plus* he can use summoners to give his enemies one-way tickets to other planes."

"Can't summoning wizards already do that?" Neera asked.

"Yes, of course..." I stopped talking.

Kami cast a speculative look at me. "What?"

Polly bustled into the bedroom carrying a fresh set of towels and a bar of soap. "That's enough excitement for now. Give the poor woman some breathing room."

The knights slowly retreated from the bed.

"The soup's ready for anyone interested," she added with a wink at me.

My visitors suddenly sprouted wings. They shot out of the room before I had a chance to say anything else.

Polly waited for the last knight to exit before speaking again. "I hope you don't mind, but I happened to overhear your conversation with your friends."

I stilled. "About the stones?"

"Before that. The dream about the meadow."

I relaxed slightly. "The subconscious is a strange place."

She nodded. "A world of its own, I agree, except I don't think you were dreaming."

I smiled. "Of course I was. There was a sunrise and a meadow." And a dead queen.

Polly set the towels on the chest of drawers and turned to face me. "I told you about my experience with monsters at the lake."

"Yes, and thank you for that." If it weren't for Polly, I wasn't sure we would've found the stone before Glendon—not that it mattered in the end.

"I've also heard other tales, ones involving alternate realities and portals." Her eyes darted to the bedroom door. "May I speak freely?"

"Of course." I sat up straighter.

"I think you were there with her."

"Where?"

"In one of those alternate planes with..." She lowered her voice. "Queen Britannia."

"The queen is dead, Polly. She was murdered twenty years ago."

"What if she wasn't?"

"Her death was confirmed by both Houses."

I thought about the alleged conspiracy to murder the

queen. What if instead of killing her, Glendon's summoners sent her to another realm? But then why wouldn't Glendon have killed her? They were at war. She was the main obstacle in his way.

My head started to pound. I drank more water.

Polly fidgeted. "What if someone saved her life by sending her through a portal—somewhere that Glendon couldn't reach?"

"Then why not get her out when the coast was clear? As you said, it happened twenty years ago."

She shrugged. "Maybe they can't. Maybe they lack the skills. Or maybe they died during the battle."

I mulled over the dream. The queen had asked for my help.

I would appreciate if you could get me out of here.

But how could I have teleported without realizing it?

"She called it her hellscape," I said.

Polly's eye twitched. "By the devil, I think she really is alive."

Even if I could get her out, I wouldn't know how to get back there. And did I want to? By all accounts, she was a vicious, power-hungry vampire. We were trying to overthrow vampire rule, not bring back its most aggressive leader.

I frowned. "It had to be a dream. I was unconscious at the lake and the stone was already gone." But its effects could have lingered. It was an ancient and powerful relic of the past and I'd formed a strong connection to it. It was no surprise if my powers went a little haywire.

Polly patted my arm. "Never mind. There's hot soup waiting for you. After what you've been through, I think that's the priority. You need your strength."

"You're very kind."

She gave me a pointed look. "Don't look so surprised. Vampires and kindness are not oxymorons. His Highness should've taught you that already."

She swept out of the room without a backward glance. On cue, my stomach churned from hunger. I peeled back the sheet and climbed out of bed. If I intended to get that stone back from Glendon, I was going to need every ounce of strength I possessed.

I gulped down the soup and returned to my bedroom where Callan was perched on the edge of the bed. He rose to his feet when I entered.

"I'm glad to see you walking around."

"I understand I have you to thank."

He looked me up and down. "How are you?"

"Good." I hobbled closer to the bed. "Almost completely healed."

"If you were less magical, you'd be dead."

"If I were less magical, I'd have been dead years ago."

He inspected my face. "Will it hurt if I kiss you?"

"Try me and find out."

It didn't hurt. Not even a little.

He broke off the kiss and leaned back. "Well?"

I frowned. "I'm not sure. Might want to try again."

He smiled and kissed me again.

I hooked my fingers around his thumbs as they caressed my cheeks. "You know your father has the stone, right?"

He offered a solemn nod. "It had to be Maeron, that idiot."

"We need to get it back."

"I thought you might say that. I've been thinking of a plan." He patted the edge of the bed and I sat beside him to listen.

As hard as I tried to focus on the stones, the image of

Britannia in the meadow continued to haunt me. I couldn't stop thinking about the possibility that the vampire queen was, in fact, trapped in another dimension where she had been for the past twenty years.

Callan cleared his throat. "You're not listening."

I snapped to attention. "Of course I am."

"Then what did I just say?"

"That your father is an ass of epic proportions and we need to get that stone. More or less."

His mouth quirked. "More or less."

I couldn't keep a secret from him. Not anymore. "There's something I need to tell you."

"Uh oh. That sounds ominous. I thought we'd cleared all the cobwebs."

"This is a new cobweb." I drew a deep breath and told him about the dream. "Say something," I urged after a prolonged silence.

He dragged a hand through his thick hair. "Britannia might be alive."

"That's what *I* said. Now you say something."

"It isn't possible."

"That's what I thought, too. Now I'm not so sure."

He wore a grim expression. "And what if she is? Then what? Release the kraken? We can't fight on two fronts. We need to get that stone from my father."

"You forgot Maeron. We're already fighting on two fronts."

He shook his head. "My brother will cave. No matter the impression he gives, he loves his family."

"So you keep telling me."

He gave me a wry smile. "Whatever we decide, we need to do it now."

I agreed. "We don't have time for travel passes. Do you

think you can convince House Lewis to let a group of us cross the border into Scotland?"

"How large of a group are we talking? Anything too obvious and you'll basically be declaring war on House Duncan."

I met his gaze. "I think we already are."

His jaw clenched.

"It's already been two days," I said. "For all we know, he might have hidden the stone by now."

"So what do you propose? We break into the castle and pry it from his cold, dead hands?"

"If we have to."

"With what army? Casek isn't going to violate the treaty. I'm not sure he fully grasps the importance of the stones."

"I think you underestimate him."

Callan's eyebrows inched up. "You want me to tell him?"

"I think we have to."

"Nobody wants war, London."

"And if we handle this right, there won't be one."

He scratched his neck. "My father will be ready for us. He'll know we're coming the second we cross the border. That's plenty of time to prepare for our arrival."

"Then maybe we won't all cross the border. Not in a way that he can see."

"Not everyone can turn invisible, London." He exhaled. "No matter what, my father will expect us to come for the stone. He'll be ready with a helluva defense."

"Then we need to make sure we're ready with a stronger offense." I hopped to my feet. "I need to make a few calls. How's the signal around here?"

"Patchy."

"I can work with that."

He grabbed my arm as I attempted to pass. "I know that expression. What's your plan? No more secrets, remember?"

My heart hammered in my chest as I looked at him. "I'll tell you, but you're not going to like it."

14

I wasn't sure how to get back to Britannia, especially because I wasn't convinced I was ever truly with her. I held to the belief that they were visions at most.

Still, if anyone was equipped to bring down Glendon, it was the former queen. It was like unleashing the velociraptors to attack the T-Rex. Maybe they'd end up killing each other.

I locked myself in the bedroom with the necessary supplies and posted Kami outside the door to keep everyone away. I drew my chalk circle, lit my candles, and set to work. At worst, I'd end up in the holiday home with the other three stones. At best, I'd find Britannia.

Nothing ventured, nothing gained.

I settled into the circle and concentrated on the meadow realm. If contact with the Summoning Stone had unlocked more of my potential, it was possible I could get myself there. I tried to recall every detail, anything to form a connection with the alternate plane and claim it as my own.

My breathing became deeper. My eyes fluttered closed and it felt like my body was tumbling through space.

When I opened my eyes again, sunlight burned my retinas and forced them closed. I shaded my brow and squinted until my eyesight adjusted.

I stood in a familiar meadow gazing at a pastel sunrise. If my visions were real, the vampire queen was here.

I walked through the meadow and let my hand skim the tops of the flowers. It was hard to believe the world had once looked like this. Bright and cheerful. Colorful. Beautiful. I continued to squint to protect my eyes from the glare of the light. I wasn't accustomed to so much of it.

I took a deep breath and tried to identify the wide range of smells. Sweet mixed with earthy, like Callan dipped in a floral-scented bathtub. Now there was a distracting thought.

A force slammed into me from behind and I pitched forward. My palms scraped the earth and I felt a light pressure on my shoulder.

"What the bloody hell?" a voice said. "Why can't my fangs penetrate this stupid suit?"

I didn't wait for her to try again. I flipped to the side and tried to knock her off. She held on like a squid sprawled around a rock.

"I think this axe is in the way." I heard the tear of fabric as she ripped the sheath. "Who carries an axe? Are you some sort of magical lumberjack?"

I threw my head backward and nailed her in the nose. The satisfying crunch of cartilage greeted my ears. I scrambled away and jumped to my feet.

Blood dripped from the queen's nose. She wore the same blood-red armor as her many statues. Her eyes glittered with menace.

She charged.

Britannia fought like a vampire who'd been trapped in

an alternate realm for twenty years and passed the time by improving her battle skills.

I punched and ducked. I avoided magic. I didn't want to kill her. I didn't even want to hurt her. For my plan to work, Britannia needed to be fully functional.

She fell backward but flipped back to her feet before I even blinked. Like Callan she proved to be preternaturally fast. All vampires were, but those like Britannia were at the top of the vampire pyramid.

"I'm not here to fight you."

She spat blood. "Aren't you an assassin sent here to finally kill me? I do appreciate they sent a woman to do the job. A man would muck it up. They always do." She sauntered a few steps closer. "What's your plan? A wooden stake through the heart? I always found that method a bit mundane."

"I'm not an assassin."

Her hands fixed to her hips. "Put down your wood chipper and prove it."

I lowered the axe to the ground, then held up my hands and returned to an upright position.

The queen examined me closely. "What trick is up your sleeve?"

Well, they nailed the paranoia part.

"No tricks. No one knows I'm here."

She exhaled. "Welcome to the club."

"I'm here because you asked me to rescue you."

Her expression changed to one of confusion. She searched my face.

"It *is* you." She laughed. It was a deep, throaty sound that seemed to emanate from the pit of her stomach. "And here I thought I invented you. I've imagined many rescuers over the years. You wouldn't be the first."

"Hopefully I'm the last."

She drank in my appearance. "You're not a vampire. What reason would you have to rescue me? I'd kill you in a heartbeat and drain every ounce of blood from your body."

I shook my head. "I don't think you will."

"I might. I'm very hungry."

"You wouldn't eat your only chance to escape."

She ripped off her helmet and tossed it to the ground. "How did you manage to find me?"

"A visit to an oracle. I seem to have forged a bridge between us."

"You're a summoner."

"Among other things." Best to omit the details for now.

"I bet you're wondering how I ended up here."

"The thought may have crossed my mind."

She dropped to the ground and sat with her knees in the air. "The truth is, I don't know."

"What's the last thing you remember?"

"The battle with that smug Highland bastard." Her head jerked up. "Did he win? Please don't tell me he's living in my palace. It took ages to get the renovations right."

"He isn't."

She whistled. "Thank the gods for small favors."

The queen had basically served a prison sentence in solitary confinement for the past twenty years.

"Do you know my son?"

"Maeron?"

She lit up at the mention of his name. "How is my sweet boy?"

I choked back laughter. "Maeron is...unique."

"He hasn't married yet, has he? I'd hate to miss all his milestones."

"He's been a bit finicky when it comes to marriage."

"Good."

"The king remarried."

"Hmm. Which trollop won the role? Let me guess. That pasty wallpaper from House Peyton? They were desperate to unite with a greater House."

"Imogen."

It took her a moment to place the name. "From across the channel? House Osmond?"

I nodded, prompting another round of throaty laughter.

"I would never have guessed her. What do you think of her?"

I shrugged. "Fine. She seems like a decent mother."

Britannia twitched. "There's another heir?"

"Her name is Davina." *And she's my sister.* "You really don't know how you got here?"

"I've had plenty of time to consider it, but no. I was too busy fighting to notice. I thought I got knocked unconscious, but I ended up here instead."

"Before I help you, we need to lay down the ground rules."

She gave me a coy look. "Ooh, now I'm intrigued. A witch laying down rules for a vampire."

"First and foremost—Davina is off limits. No harming her to solidify Maeron as the only heir or to hurt Imogen or Casek."

She arched an eyebrow. "The intrigue grows. Girlfriend?"

"Sister."

The vampire's face rippled with confusion. "You're Imogen's daughter?"

"No." I watched and waited. Eventually she seemed to grasp the implication.

She exhaled. "I suppose I shouldn't be surprised. How old are you?"

"Thirty."

"And yet you claim he hasn't sent you here? Do you expect me to believe you?"

"Trust isn't built in a day, so no."

"I believe that was Rome, darling." She scrutinized me. "You have his eyes. I see that now."

"You don't seem too bothered by my species."

"I've been imprisoned for twenty years, darling. You tend to shift your priorities." She gave me a sly look. "Now I know who your mother is. The pretty teacher who came to the palace. I noticed her first, but I saw the way Casek looked at her and I backed off."

She knew. Queen Britannia knew.

"You weren't jealous of another woman with your husband?"

She snorted. "As much as I preferred to be the center of the universe, I could hardly blame him. I like men well enough, but I much prefer the company of women. My job was to produce an heir, which I did, and a son to boot. Duty fulfilled." She dusted off her hands.

I started to understand the king's relationship with my mother a bit better.

"Did you have anyone special in your life?"

"Who's more special than me? I'm quite content with my own company." She glanced around her. "Well, I was. I think it's somewhat unreasonable to expect me not to crave the company of others after all this time alone."

"Agreed."

"Is he with her now—your mother? Does poor Imogen mind?"

"My mother died many years ago. She never told me who my father was. She thought it would keep me safe."

Her full lips formed a pout. "There's no such thing as safe. I feel quite confident you've learned that lesson by now, haven't you?"

"Yes." I took no pleasure in admitting it though.

A strong, confident woman. No wonder Britannia was Glendon's biggest threat. He couldn't handle being beaten by her. He would've been just as happy to control her as to kill her. As it turned out, he managed neither. But what about Casek? What was my father's role in this? Did he even have one?

The queen raised her chin a fraction, regarding me. "I'm glad it's you. I'd hate to be rescued by a man. Utter humiliation." She folded her arms around her knees. "So, where do we start?"

I pushed up my sleeves. "With a story about a wizard named Friseal."

I finished the story—the whole story, including my visit to the Atheneum. Britannia was quiet, appearing to digest it all.

"So, what do you think?"

The vampire queen idly flicked the stem of a nearby flower. "I'm not sure."

"What aren't you sure about?"

"Perhaps it's best if I don't return."

I balked. "Why? Your greatest enemy is still alive. Your son misses you."

"After everything you've told me, I wonder whether there's no longer a place for me in that world. Perhaps I should find another one more suited to me."

I frowned. "But you were so eager for me to rescue you."

"It's what I've dreamed of every day for twenty years."

She sighed. "But now that the prospect is here, I don't know anymore. Casek has a queen. My son is grown. I have no land to rule over. I don't feel like I belong anywhere."

Now wasn't the time for an existential crisis. I needed her strength. Still, I couldn't force her.

"How about this? I'm going to return to my realm now because I have work to do, but I'll leave this door unlocked for you."

Her brow furrowed. "You can do that?"

I shrugged. "It might be tricky since I didn't create this place, but I seem to have claimed it as mine so…"

"A tentative yes." She cocked her head and studied me. "I can see why we've been so threatened by your kind."

"Not all dhampirs are created equal in terms of power. Anyway, it's what we do with that power that matters."

A hint of a smile passed her lips. "And you intend to save the world with it?"

"Or die trying."

She nodded. "You remind me of my younger self."

"In what way?"

"After the Great Eruption, when night fell, I saw an opportunity and I seized it with both fangs. What others saw as a Napoleon-style power grab, I viewed as the start of a new era in our world's history. The old world was complete rubbish. I long believed vampires could do a better job at the helm than humans."

"Do you still believe that?"

"As you can imagine, I've had quite a long time to consider the question. I don't think it's the species that matters so much as the character of those in positions of leadership."

"There was a time I would've disagreed with you." Not

very long ago, in fact, but meeting Callan changed the way I viewed vampires.

She smiled at me. "And what say you now, dhampir?"

"I say that Glendon is not the type of vampire that should be in a position of power." I hesitated. "Can I ask you something else? I've heard so much about you." So much that didn't seem to fit with the vampire currently seated beside me. "The churches...Why did you destroy them?"

Britannia plucked a white flower from the ground and twirled it lightly in front of her nose. "Wouldn't you have done the same in my position? The churches weren't exactly kind to vampires over the centuries, nor to women, and I was both."

"Then it was revenge?"

"No, not revenge. I wanted to change the world, mold it to my vision. That was just one of many steps."

I glanced at her. "And now? How would you describe your vision?"

"I'm not sure, but I would very much like to see my son again."

"I'm sure he feels the same."

She tossed the flower to the ground. "I'll consider your proposal."

I rose to my feet. I'd made my pitch. There was nothing more to say. "Thank you, Your Majesty."

She laughed. "Save your title. I haven't been a queen in twenty years. I'm Britannia Lewis now. Not as impressive, but I've come to like her very much. I'd even go as far as to say I love her."

I gazed at her. "I have to admit, this did not go the way I expected."

She offered a weak smile. "Things rarely do."

Disappointment bloomed in my chest. It was hard to

return to my realm, knowing I couldn't rely on her support. Twenty years in solitary confinement had obviously altered her. How could it not? She possessed the physical skills, but if she no longer possessed the killer instinct or the thirst for power, then my efforts here were in vain. On the other hand, I'd given her the option of leaving her ivory tower. If nothing else, I'd set her free. What she opted to do with that freedom was her choice, as it should be.

15

K ami pounced on me the moment I opened the bedroom door at Alnwick Castle. "How'd it go?"

My eyes adjusted to the change in light. "It went."

She peered behind me. "Where is she?"

"Still deciding."

"How can she still be deciding? I thought she was desperate for someone to let her out of her cage."

"We had a nice chat. She wants time to consider the offer."

Kami stared at me with her mouth hanging open. "What's in that realm? A harem of washboard abs and an endless supply of wine and chocolate?"

"Meadows. Many, many meadows."

She pinched my sleeve. "Are you telling me that Queen Britannia, the fiercest vampire in the history of vampires, has become a hippie?"

I shrugged. "Stranger things have happened. I'll tell you what, though, she's in the greatest shape of her life. She could've killed me before I said a word."

"In that case, I'm glad she became a hippie." She held up

a finger. "But only in that case."

"We'll have to carry out our plan without her."

"It was a long shot anyway."

Callan strode into the room and my heart skipped a beat. "Agreed."

I met his gaze. "You heard all that?"

"I did. Part of me wishes I could've been there to see it for myself. I have a hard time believing she didn't leap at the chance to return here and seek vengeance."

"She isn't the same vampire. To be honest, I don't think she was ever the vampire everyone made her out to be."

"You don't think she was trying to pull the wool over your eyes?" he asked.

"For what purpose? I offered her a deal that involved letting loose the vampire I learned about, not the one I met in the meadow."

His expression grew wistful. "I wish I believed my father was capable of that kind of change."

I smiled. "Maybe they can swap places. We'll throw Glendon in the meadow realm and check on him in twenty years."

He sighed. "We'd need to evacuate Britannia first or they'd end up killing each other over the boundaries of the rose bushes."

"She wants to see Maeron. If anything motivates her to abandon her prison, it will be the desire to see her son."

Callan frowned. "What if you brought him there?"

I laughed. "Do you honestly think Maeron would trust me enough to accompany me? He'd think it was a trap."

"Fair enough. So, what now?"

"We proceed with the plan. We've got a great team, with or without Britannia."

He nodded. "That we do. On that note, my father has arrived."

I snapped to attention. "The king is here?"

"He insisted. He's outraged and wants to be involved."

I cast a wary glance at the empty doorway. "Perfect timing then."

He angled his head. "Your face says otherwise."

"Now that he's here, there's something I should do."

Kami touched my shoulder. "You don't have to."

I twisted to look at her. "You've always told me to open up and let everyone know the real me. If I'm going to fight for House Lewis beside its king, I need to have this conversation first."

"Are you sure Maeron hasn't already told him?" Kami asked.

"It's a possibility, but I won't know unless I say something."

Callan's face tightened. "If he lays a hand on you…"

I looked up at him. "Listen, this is as much a tactical decision as an emotional one. Casek needs me right now. He doesn't want that stone in your father's hands either. It's the optimum time to come clean."

He cupped the back of my head and pressed his forehead against mine. "Even off the battlefield, you're a force to be reckoned with, London Hayes."

Kami rubbed the sides of her arms. "Oh, wow. Do you two need a moment? I suddenly feel like a creeper."

We broke apart.

"Wish me luck," I said, and exited the room.

I found the king in the banquet hall, seated at the twenty-foot-long table. Alone in the cavernous room, he looked comically small.

Sensing a presence, he glanced up from the paperwork in front of him. "London, how nice to see you again."

"Busy?"

He signed the top sheet of paper. "A king's work is never done, I'm afraid. A hazard of the job. It doesn't help that I'm not in my own office. I like routine and consistency, although this castle is nicer than I remember." With an airy wave, he motioned to the chair adjacent to his. "Please sit."

"I'd rather stand, if you don't mind, Your Majesty."

He examined me. "Something on your mind?"

"There is."

"I must thank you for alerting me to the stone. I promise you, we'll find a way to recover it. We've beaten Glendon before and we can do it again."

"I don't want to ignite a war."

"Nor do I, which is why I'm not calling upon my army. This mission will be kept as quiet as possible."

I cleared my throat. It was now or never. "I'm not here about the stone, Your Majesty."

He set down the pen. "Then what is it?"

I searched his face for any hint of knowledge but saw nothing. Maeron hadn't told him. The prince hadn't told anyone. I couldn't decide whether it was because he didn't believe it or he didn't want to believe it. Either way, that meant the king was oblivious to our familial connection.

I drew a shaky breath. Nothing my mother told me had prepared me for this moment.

"You once knew a witch called Rhea. Once upon a time she demonstrated magic to children at the palace."

He stared at me. "Yes, of course."

My stomach tightened. "I'm her daughter."

His expression remained neutral. "I see. Married a man named Hayes, did she?"

"No. It was the name she used to raise me."

"Is she well, your mother?"

And there it was. A hopeful intonation. The inflection that told me he loved her still.

"She died many years ago."

His shoulders sagged. "I'm sorry. A terrible loss. And your father?"

"He seems well, although he's about to go into battle with a monster." I inclined my head toward the table. "And he seems overly committed to bureaucracy."

The king's hands dropped to his sides and he leaned against the back of the chair. "I don't understand."

I clasped my hands in front of me. "I'm your daughter, Your Majesty."

Shock registered on his face. "Daughter?"

"She feared for my life, so she decided the best course of action was to hide my existence. She raised me as a witch. She trained me to develop my abilities but also to hide them."

The king rubbed his hand over his face. "Not only your abilities. She hid you from me."

"Surely you can understand why."

He appeared slightly dazed. "Did she truly believe I would murder our child?"

"Why wouldn't you? I'm a dhampir. It's illegal for me to exist."

"And yet you come to me now and declare yourself. Why?"

"Because I'm not my mother and I'm not a child anymore." I took a step closer. "And I'm not afraid of you."

He looked at me intently. "Your eyes. I'd noticed them before…It didn't occur to me." He chuckled. "Even Imogen commented on them."

"I haven't known about you my whole life. I only discovered the truth recently. My mother refused to tell me your identity. She only told me you were a vampire and that it made me a hunted species."

Slowly the king rose to his feet. His gaze never left my face. "I see the commonalities now. Your eyes are like mine, but your face is hers."

"With all due respect, Your Majesty, my face is my own."

He bowed his head. "Yes, of course."

I lifted my chin, almost daring him. "Are you going to have me executed?"

He seemed stunned by the question. "I...I don't know. I don't see how I could do such a thing."

"If you can't do it to me, then you shouldn't do it at all. It shouldn't matter that I'm your daughter."

The king frowned. "There are rules for a reason."

"Yes, and I'm the reason. Make no mistake, Your Majesty. I am powerful, more than you know, and I intend to use that power to help defeat Glendon and take the stone. But you can't have it both ways. You can't condemn me for my power while also benefitting from it."

"You think I should repeal the law."

"Yes."

He studied my face. "I thought I had only my memories of us, yet there's been evidence of our love in the world all this time."

"Thirty years, precisely."

He rubbed his chin. "I must confess, I'm not entirely sure how to behave. Davina would throw her arms around you and welcome you to the family." His eyebrows shot up. "Does she know?"

"Not yet. I thought you should be told first." I hesitated. "But Callan and Maeron know."

He sniffed. "And yet they kept it from me."

"You can understand their reasons."

"Callan, maybe, but not Maeron."

"I think he was deciding how the information would be most beneficial to him."

He wagged a finger at me. "Now that sounds like my son."

My heart beat rapidly. "I'm glad I got the chance to tell you the truth."

"The burden of a secret like that is no small matter. It must've weighed on you."

"I'm used to secrets." Although I had to admit, the more I revealed them, the lighter I felt.

He continued to gaze at me. "If you don't mind me asking, how did she die?"

"An infection. By the time we discovered it, she was beyond healers. If it helps you at all, there wasn't anyone else in her life after you. I used to believe it was because of our secret, that she couldn't bring herself to trust anyone, but now I think it was also because she never stopped loving you."

Tears glistened in his eyes. "It's been much the same for me. A lonely road to walk. If not for my children, I would've been lost." A faint smile emerged. "My children," he repeated, this time more to himself. "Davina is on her way here. Would it be all right with you if I told her? It seems right that the news should come from me."

"I thought you might say that. Yes, I think it should be as well."

"Where do we go from here?"

"I think you'll agree the stone is the priority, but I don't want a war with House Duncan. Everyone will suffer if that happens."

"Everyone will suffer if he controls the stone. As soon as he figures out how to send all his competition to other realms, you're as good as gone." *Like your wife*, I nearly said, but kept my mouth shut.

The king's face hardened. "He was always a wily bastard. As I said, I'd like to keep our party as small as possible. I don't want subjects to think we're there to claim Scotland. I have no interest in ruling it."

"Define small."

"An elite squad."

"I can help with that."

He smiled. "I thought you might."

I turned to leave so he could be alone with his thoughts.

"She'd be damn proud of you, you know. Damn proud."

I pushed down the lump in my throat and looked at him. "Thank you."

The other knights were gathered in the kitchen. They'd assembled a layout of Glendon's castle using salt and pepper shakers, a spatula, and an assortment of other household items.

"Very professional," I remarked.

Kami glanced up. "Callan helped."

"We need a diversion that's convincing enough to draw out Glendon's most powerful line of defense," I said. "We need him to believe we're hitting him with everything we've got."

"Then I'll go." Callan appeared behind me. "He won't expect any son of his to be part of the B team."

Davina ran into the kitchen, already barefoot. Her gaze darted from knight to knight. When her gaze landed on me, she laughed gleefully. The sound was joy personified.

"Is it true?"

"Yes."

She rushed forward and threw her arms around me. Hugging didn't come naturally to me. I gave her back an awkward pat.

"I wanted to tell you," I said.

She pressed her cheek against my chest. "I don't care what you are or any stupid law. I won't let anyone punish you for existing."

"Thank you, Davina." I hadn't expected to feel so relieved. I gave her an extra squeeze before releasing her.

"Whose idea was it for you to come?" Callan asked, sliding into my place for a hug. "We're about to…"

Davina folded her arms. "I know what you're about to do. Why do you think I hurried to catch up to Father?"

"You cannot join us," Callan said. "Your mother has been left in control of Buckingham Palace. You can stay here and look after Alnwick."

Davina stifled a laugh. "You're joking. You can't possibly think I'd be willing to sit home when you're all off on a grand adventure."

"It isn't an adventure, Davina."

My whole body stiffened at the sound of Maeron's voice. Callan immediately stepped between us.

"What are you doing here, brother?" Callan demanded.

He puffed out his chest. "My family is about to go into battle. Where else would I be?" He seemed to notice the knights surrounding the table. "Well, well. The gang's all here."

Someone snarled. Most likely Kami.

"Give us the Immortality Stone and we'll consider it." Callan held out his hand.

"I told you before, it's perfectly safe. I only took it so that Glendon's witch couldn't. I knew he'd send someone sooner or later. The clock was ticking."

"Where is it then? Where have you hidden it?" I asked.

Davina muscled her way into the middle. "Please don't fight. There's enough of that on the horizon."

Maeron's eyes flashed with anger. "How do we know Callan won't betray us at the first opportunity? Glendon *is* his father."

I barked a laugh. "Callan? If this is your attempt to misdirect us, Your Highness, you're failing miserably. We all know who the real traitor is here."

Davina clasped Callan's hand. "He's as much my brother as you are. I trust him with my life."

Maeron threw up his hands and stalked out of the room.

Kami raised her hand. "Your Highness...Your Highnessi? Highnesses?" She scrunched her nose. "What's the plural? Anyway, I have to be honest, we're not entirely comfortable riding into battle with someone who tried to kill us."

Davina spun toward her. "He'll get it together, I promise. He's been like this from the time I was a little girl."

I looked at her. "Temperamental and untrustworthy?"

"A jackass?" Kami added.

Davina observed the empty space where Maeron had been standing. "Whenever he's being prickly, I try to remind myself how I would feel if my mother had been the one to die."

There was no point in mentioning Britannia—not to Davina or Casek and certainly not to Maeron. If the former queen opted to keeping playing dead, it was best not to reopen old wounds.

"When do we leave for Scotland?" Davina asked.

Callan groaned. "Davina, stop. There's no 'we.'"

Using her head as a battering ram, she launched herself at the vampire. Her head crashed into the vulnerable part of his abdomen and down he went. Her fangs gleamed as she straddled him and withdrew a dagger from hiding. With lightning speed, she grabbed his arm as he raised it to unseat her.

"I didn't ask permission. I am joining the fight and that's the end of it."

Callan's head dropped back to the floor. "Fine."

She gaped at him. "Really?"

"You said you weren't asking."

The mask of a badass princess fell back into place. "I'm not." She slid off him and returned to her feet.

Callan resumed a standing position. "There's one condition. You're riding with the third wave."

She swiveled to face the knights. "What's that?"

Neera stepped forward, mother hen that she was. "I'm leading the third wave. You can ride with me." She motioned to Davina's dagger. "If you're going to fight, though, you need more than one small blade." She glanced down at Davina's bare feet. "And shoes might help."

I glanced at Callan. "I assume you have an armory somewhere in this place."

"Morris will show her. Come on. I'll take you to him."

"Do you have a katana?" Davina asked as he guided her away. "I've always wanted to wield one."

Callan glanced at me over his shoulder and winked.

It would take more than a katana and a sunny disposition to win this battle.

A helluva lot more.

16

"Where does King Casek keep his armies?" Kami popped her hands into view. "In his sleevies." Morris's grandchildren burst into laughter.

"Now out of here, you lot," Polly ordered. "The adults are busy." She ushered them from the kitchen with the sweep of a broom.

"I think you found your calling," I told Kami.

Kami shrugged. "I like kids, but I don't think mother-hood is in the cards for me. Maybe in a different world."

"That different world might be here sooner than you think."

Ione stared at the table, where household objects still laid out our strategy. "Is the king sure he doesn't want to call upon his army? Because this is starting to look like a suicide mission."

"I made a few calls," I said.

"And?" Stevie prompted.

"And they said they'd consider it."

"Can't the king command them?" Briar asked.

"That's not how he's choosing to handle this." And I had to admit, I respected him for it. "I'm calling in favors."

"I'd rather call in an army," Ione mumbled.

Morris entered the kitchen and bowed. "You're wanted in the banquet hall."

Kami's gaze swept the room. "Who?"

"All of you."

We abandoned the table and headed for the banquet hall.

Joseph Yardley sat at the long table with an entourage. I recognized some of the witches and wizards I'd met at the PSR meeting.

"I hope you don't mind that I brought reinforcements," the wizard said. "It seems to me we're all in this together."

I examined him. "And by that, you mean that we're going to fight together and you're not going to try to smuggle the stone out of there for your own purposes."

The wizard smiled. "Do you think I'm truly that devious?"

"I think you're truly that single-minded."

"Then why ask for our assistance?"

"Because we need you. It's that simple."

"You have my word, Miss Hayes."

I took the seat adjacent to him. "Good, because I have a plan."

The group spent the next two hours discussing next steps and resolving a few disagreements about tactics. Everyone was an expert in this group. They just didn't necessarily agree on how to execute that expertise. Much of the discussion involved where Glendon would keep the stone.

"I suspect he'll carry it himself," Callan said. "His paranoia is both a weakness and a strength. He won't trust anyone else not to use it against him, especially his summoners. They're paid staff. I'm not sure how loyal they would be if they could overpower him."

"That seems like an advantage for us," Ione said.

Callan looked at her. "Maybe so, but he'll also be surrounded by his fiercest warriors."

King Casek inclined his head toward me. "And so will I."

"You're B team, remember," I told him. "Let Glendon think you're the one coming for the stone." He'd never suspect that the king would be willing to relegate himself to the secondary team. Glendon's ego was another thing we had in our favor.

The king pivoted toward Callan. "And what do you think will be waiting for us in Scotland?"

The vampire's expression turned grim. "The fight of our lives."

The king nodded. "Then let's make it count."

Weapons were distributed and tasks assigned. Polly walked through the room with bottles of blood for the vampires and food for the rest of us.

The king took a long drink and then scrutinized the bottle. "This is excellent, Callan. Where'd you get it?"

"A conversation for a later time," Callan said. I didn't miss the hint of a smile on his face.

Everyone departed the castle for the Scottish border at the same time. Each team had its own orders once we crossed the border.

"Yardley, you're up," I said.

Callan swaggered over to me. "That's my cue."

I placed my palms flat on his chest and stood on my toes to kiss him. "Stay safe."

"No chance of that."

I kissed him again. "Then stay alive."

"Same to you."

He reluctantly peeled himself away from me as the Green Wizard gathered the B team and prepared to teleport. He raised his hand. Nothing happened. His brow furrowed.

"Is there a problem, Yardley?" the king asked.

"There's a blockage, Your Majesty."

"What does that mean? You need to clear your mind?"

"No," Yardley said. "It means that King Glendon has put up a ward that prevents anyone from teleporting across the border."

The king sighed. "Well, I suppose I shouldn't be surprised. After all, he knows we're coming."

"This plan is off to a roaring good start," Maeron said. "What do you suggest now? We all go home and hope for the best?"

"You'd like that, wouldn't you?" Kami said. "Give your partner-in-crime a chance to secure the stone."

The king's brow creased. "What does she mean, Maeron?"

He ducked his head and scowled. "Nothing."

"We have loads of witches and wizards with us," Davina said. "Surely they're capable of breaking the ward."

Murmurs rippled through the group.

"We can try, Your Highness," Yardley said. "But it will take time."

We didn't have the luxury of time. There was no point in hiding my abilities anymore. I approached the border and pulled out my dagger.

"Everybody ready," I yelled. I sliced the blade across my palm and let my blood drip to the ground. I felt resistance and squeezed a few more drops. The magic bucked but eventually yielded.

Davina stared at me, wide-eyed. "You broke it?"

"Only part of it." But part of it was all we needed.

Yardley poofed, along with his team.

"Can my blood do that?" Davina asked. She prepared to sink her fangs into her wrist, but I stopped her.

"Your blood won't have the same effect."

"Can't I at least try?"

"There will be enough blood spilled today. Let's not lose any more than necessary."

She smiled and lowered her arm. "You're right, sister."

Neera joined us and put an arm around Davina. "C team is ready."

I nodded. "The ward is down. Let's go."

B team had teleported to Glendon's castle. Their job was to keep the king's defenders occupied and wear them down in anticipation of our arrival. If all went according to plan, Glendon would stay focused on his royal rivals and ignore the rest of us.

The witches and wizards remaining behind used elemental magic to speed up our journey. Between the wind at our backs and using the earth as a flat escalator, we made better time than I calculated. We were only five miles from the castle when a man cloaked in the colors of House Duncan appeared out of nowhere and blocked our path.

"Are you the welcome committee?" Kami called. "Because I could really do with a drink."

He pressed his hands together in prayer form and I felt the waves of magic pulsing through the air.

"A summoner," someone yelled.

I withdrew my axe and tensed for the outcome.

Red and orange light sparked and formed a glowing circle. I took a hesitant step backward. The circle continued to expand until the circumference was about six feet. A creature launched itself through the red portal. Large paws landed on the earth with a heavy thud. A gryphon.

The wizard pointed at me.

There wasn't time to play nice. I reached out and seized the gryphon's mind. I usually preferred a gentler approach, but every second counted.

The gryphon resisted. I pushed harder. I felt like I was trying to ride a mechanical bull. The gryphon thrashed and tried in vain to buck me from his head.

I won.

I took control of the gryphon and turned the creature toward the wizard. The fear in his eyes told me he realized what I'd done.

"How?" he whispered.

"Is this where you beg me to teach you my ways? I don't think so."

"I've heard of such abilities but have never seen it with my own eyes."

"You'll have a lot time to think about it."

The gryphon lifted the wizard into the air and sailed into the portal. The lights died and the circle dissipated.

"Only one summoner?" Kami said. "That's a disappointment."

There was no sign of anyone else. I checked my phone to see whether there was a message from Callan.

Terrific. A message from an hour ago. Damn satellites.

Only defenders at the castle. Heading to hunting lodge.

Where was the king's hunting lodge?

"What's the matter?" Davina asked.

"Glendon isn't here. Callan thinks he's taken the stone to his hunting lodge."

Davina beamed. "Oh, Balmoral. I've heard it's grand."

Balmoral. My mother had told me about Balmoral

Castle, which had belonged to the Windsors, the last royal human family before the Great Eruption.

"North," I announced. "We need to travel north."

Unfortunately Glendon's soldiers had other plans.

Vampires streamed toward us as though someone had turned on a faucet.

"More summoners," Kami said.

Yardley's team was able to teleport out quickly. We wouldn't be so lucky.

"Demons!" Davina yelled.

I heard a tinge of excitement in her voice. I was glad somebody was happy about this. Even so, I shoved her behind me. "Neera, stay with the princess."

I ignored the cries of protest as I sprinted forward. The demons were unfamiliar to me, which made them harder to fight. They sported razor-sharp claws, bodies covered in coarse black hair, pointy ears, and red eyes that glowed. The eyes were creepy but it also made them easy to spot in the shadows.

I wasn't sure whether the demons were intended to be the starters or the main course. No matter how many I fought, there seemed to be more ready to take their place. Demons seemed to rain down from the sky. It had to be the summoners.

My skin was so slick with blood that the axe slipped from my hand. As I bent to retrieve it, another demon jumped on my back. Its claws scraped against my magical armor, but the material held firm. I tried to flip forward and throw the demon to the ground, but its claws dug in. It had clearly attended the Queen Britannia School of Fighting.

I decided to fall backward instead. The sudden move took the demon by surprise and the claws retracted long enough for me to escape its clutches. I scurried toward Babe on my hands and knees, but the demon was faster. It grasped the handle of the axe and lifted it over its hideous head. A bullet whizzed past me and nailed the demon between the eyes. The creature seemed as shocked as I did before it slumped to the ground, unmoving. Babe landed on the ground beside it.

I turned to see Mack lowering a rifle. In the background I counted a dozen knights from his banner already in the thick of it.

They came. I didn't know why I was so shocked by their arrival—I'd called them for help, but still. This wasn't their fight. This wasn't their job.

But they were here anyway.

Mack grinned. "You're welcome, Hayes." He jerked to his left to shoot an incoming demon.

I swept Babe off the ground and ran.

I seemed to face off against every creature known to man and others I didn't know existed. Land hydras. Flying monkeys. Giant serpents with tusks. Glendon must've ordered his summoners to pull out all the stops. Whatever it took to keep us from getting to Balmoral. Well, it was working. If this kept up, the B team was going to have to become the A team.

Kami limped over to me. Her blond hair was matted with blood and her crossbow was broken. "We're getting our asses kicked."

"He's more prepared than I realized."

"And he's using the stone. I don't think his summoners could've gotten all these creatures here without help."

A vicious snarl forced my attention to the left. I lifted a hand, ready to blow the creature backward. Before I could act, a wolf jumped from the side and toppled the demon.

Out of the corner of my eye, two more wolves were tearing the heads off a land hydra.

"Where the hell did all these wolves come from?" Kami asked.

A man jogged across the field, looking left to right. "I'm looking for London Hayes."

I raised a hand. "That's me."

He offered his hand and I shook it. "Paul Whitmore from the Cumbrian Pack. The West End Wolf Pack said you might need a hand."

My spirits soared.

"How many?"

"I've got three dozen wolves with me and another hundred or so en route from the other northern counties."

So much for a small and secret mission.

"What about the ward?" Kami asked.

"Ward's down. We made it across with no trouble."

Kami nudged me. "Look at you, Miss Modesty. And you thought you only broke part of it."

"Thank you," I said.

Paul nodded. "We're all in this together. Anything particular we need to know?"

I told him about King Glendon at Balmoral.

He rolled up his sleeves. "We can handle things, if you want to make your way there." He let loose a shrill whistle and then transformed to join the melee as a wolf.

It was time for my own transformation. I peeled off versions of myself one layer at a time and sent them into battle. It was liberating not to hide my magic. I was a much more effective fighter when I could use all the weapons in my arsenal.

And there were many.

My phone vibrated and I tugged it out of my suit. Another message from Callan.

You need to get here. Now.

My stomach plummeted. I had to find a faster way to get there. I spotted Kami who seemed content to watch two wizards take turns smacking each other in the face. She noticed me and gave me a sheepish grin.

"Mind control doesn't have to be boring."

"Stop playing and help me get to Balmoral. Callan said they need help."

She pointed skyward. "You need to hitch a ride."

"Birds can't hold my weight."

"I'm not talking about birds."

I looked up as a horde of dragons passed overhead. In the gloaming, they looked like an enormous misshapen cloud.

I reached out and tried to identify the weakest mind. Bingo. I formed a connection and urged the dragon toward me. I couldn't tell whether I'd been successful until I saw a shadow peel away from the moving black glob. Screams pierced the air around me, but I kept my focus on coaxing the dragon to the ground.

"We need more wolves," Stevie panted, breaking my connection. "I just watched two get carried off by flying monkeys."

The dragon hovered in the air, uncertain what just happened.

Don't go.

"How many of you are there, London?" Ione asked. "I think I counted six."

"Not enough."

"Beast Briar just took down a giant serpent by herself," Ione said.

More shrieks hurt my ears. A dozen winged monkeys swooped from the shadows. I sliced Babe through the air before they could sink their claws into me. They were too close in range for Ione's arrows and too high in the air for her earth magic.

I started to feel suffocated. Their wings smacked my head as they made another attempt to snatch me off the ground.

The sound of hoofbeats radiated in my chest and the hair on the back of my neck pricked. More vampires. I sliced the wing from a monkey and that was when I spotted a figure in blood-red armor cutting through the mist. The helmet left the lower half of her face visible.

Not more vampires plural. Only one.

Silence fell over the field. It seemed that even the other-worldly creatures knew the tide was about to turn.

"It can't be," someone said.

Britannia raised her sword in the air and yelled, "All right, my lovelies. Who's interested in dying today?"

Chaos erupted.

Every slice. Every blow. Her smile remained intact. The vampire queen was in her element. I only knew of her skills on the battlefield through secondhand accounts, but I was convinced she'd improved tenfold since then. There were certain advantages to spending two decades alone in a hellscape. True to form, Britannia hadn't wasted them.

Kami ran past me and slowed to a trot. "Holy hellfire, is that her?"

"It is."

"She actually came. You did it, London." Kami swung a club at an approaching vampire and hit him squarely in the temple. He staggered to the side and fell.

"Since when do you use a club?" I asked.

"Since ten minutes ago. Its owner died and it was just sitting there looking at me all pathetic." The vampire got up and she hit him again.

I blasted a trio of approaching ogres with a gust of air and they blew off their feet.

"More keep coming," Kami said. "It's like he keeps opening fresh jars of minions."

I whistled at Stevie and she jogged over, ducking as an ogre went sailing over her head.

"You need to find the wizard or witch that's bringing in the fresh troops and put a stop to it."

She saluted me. "I'll bring Briar with me."

"No. Neera and Ione." Briar was in full beast mode and I didn't want to lose her on the field.

"What about Davina?" Stevie asked.

"Send her to me."

"Got it." She dashed across the field toward the sisters.

A primal yell reverberated. Britannia was having fun. Good. If anyone deserved a good time, it was the lonely vampire queen.

Davina appeared beside me, looking remarkably adorable for a teen vampire in the middle of a battle. Even her clothing was intact and unstained. Impressive.

"Is that who I think it is?" she asked. Her gaze was pinned on Britannia.

"It is."

"Wow," she breathed. "Mother's going to have a coronary."

"Not if Britannia has one first."

I glanced up and saw my ride was still waiting. I reforged a connection and urged him to the ground. Once the dragon was close enough, I was able to see the creature clearly. Green scales. Orange flash. A fire breather. Perfect.

Davina backed away. "What are you doing?"

"Hitching a ride and you're coming with me."

Her eyes rounded. "You want me to ride a dragon?" She didn't wait for an answer. "This is the best day ever!"

"Hey, buddy," I said in a soothing tone. "I'm London and I'll be your pilot today."

I edged closer and kept my hand out with my palm up. The dragon lowered his head and shocked me by flicking out a forked tongue and licking my hand.

Slowly I moved to his bulky side and climbed aboard. Then I held out a hand for Davina.

"We're off to see the wizard," I sang.

Lots of them.

The dragon soared north into the great black yonder.

Up ahead I spotted a group of shadows moving at a fast pace ahead. Glendon's reinforcements.

Gotcha.

I touched the dragon's mind and felt around for the right button.

Ready. Steady.

"Now!"

I directed the dragon to dive-bomb the troops as fire streamed from his mouth.

Davina whooped. "This is amazing!"

Once the fire hit the ground, I bent and shaped the flames until they formed a circle that contained the troops.

One of the elemental wizards managed to break through the flames using a water spout and they spilled out into the darkness.

If at first we don't succeed, then try, try again.

I turned the dragon back for another attempt, but the troops decided to go on the offensive. Flame-tipped arrows flew toward us, skimming the dragon's wings and sides. One narrowly missed the heel of my boot.

I pressed on.

My body tensed as the silhouette of Balmoral came into view. A ring of fire burned around the perimeter of the building, whether to keep people in or out, I wasn't sure. I had to find Callan and the others.

"Hold on," I instructed Davina. "This landing might be a bit bumpy."

THE DRAGON LANDED on the interior of the fiery wall. My boots hit the ground with a soft thud.

A blast of air sent me sailing back through the firewall. Groaning, I climbed to my feet and walked straight back through the flames. Whoever hit me didn't know about my immunity to fire. Surprise!

Davina stared at me in wonder. "How?"

"Generations of mixed DNA and I got all the lucky genes." I grabbed her by the hand. "Let's go."

We ran around the side of the building in search of the others. We found them at the back. B Team had managed to position themselves between Glendon and Balmoral, effectively blocking his entrance. The ring of fire prevented the king from escaping into the woods. Unfortunately there were still skilled defenders between our team and the king, although they were comprised of fewer monsters and more vampires and wizards. I spotted Murdina among them and glowered. The traitorous witch glared back at me.

"London!" Callan's relief was palpable.

I rushed over to join the fray and immediately noticed the king's midsection. "Is he wearing a fanny pack?"

Callan smirked as he punched an attacker. "It's where he's keeping the stone."

"That's just insulting to the ancient artifact." If I were the stone, I'd implode just out of spite.

"Davina, stay back," King Casek ordered when he spotted her.

She unsheathed her katana. "Absolutely, Father. Whatever you say."

This was Glendon's final wall of defense. If we could get past them, we could recover the stone.

A winged shadow passed overhead and a figure dropped to the ground with aplomb. Her helmet was gone and her hair flowed behind her in soft waves. The blood-red armor shone like a ruby in the night sky.

Casek turned with a sword in his hand. His jaw slackened and the weapon dropped to his side. "Gods have mercy. Britannia?"

"Hello, husband. We can catch up later. I believe we have other priorities at the moment." She blew him a kiss and faced the rest of Glendon's defenders.

Maeron stood paralyzed and gaped at her.

Britannia's gaze landed on the prince. "Look at you, Maeron. How handsome. Now let's see what your father has taught you in my absence. Make your mum proud."

There was no time for a proper reunion. The arrival of Britannia gave the defenders renewed strength. Glendon bellowed commands from behind them. His face was red with rage.

"Protect the king," someone yelled and I wasn't sure which king they meant.

Glendon's reinforcements had arrived.

We were outnumbered.

I shifted the ground and watched opponents topple. I

pushed the air and watched them tumble. Magic poured from me effortlessly like water from a jug. I'd never been granted this much freedom before. I knew it was dangerous. Maintaining that balance had been a crucial part of my training. As much magic as I flung at them, more came at me.

Where were the knights? They clearly hadn't located the source of the running tap of minions. I tried not to worry. They were the most competent witches I knew. If there was a way to succeed, they'd find it.

One by one, the defenders were dispatched until only Glendon remained. My father's arm hung limp and blood streaked from injuries I couldn't identify.

Maeron was closest to the Highland king. He surged ahead.

"Maeron, you don't want to do this," Glendon said. "If you want power, son, you only need to stand with me. You have the Immortality Stone. I have the Summoning Stone. Together we can rule the world."

Casek's face darkened. "Don't you dare call him son."

"You tried to murder his mother," Davina yelled. "You don't have the right."

"And failed miserably, I might add." Britannia stomped over a dead body on her way toward them.

Laughter bubbled from Glendon's throat. "If I don't have the right to call him son because of that, then neither does he." His gaze drifted to Casek. "After all, it takes two to conspire."

"My hands are clean," Casek said.

"Only because I did your dirty work for you and then you betrayed me. You promised me the Immortality Stone!"

Davina looked up at her father. "I don't understand."

Maeron swiveled to face us, his face somber. "I do." He

locked eyes with his father. "You struck a deal with Glendon. You agreed to give him the stone and let him murder my mother if he called off the invasion."

"And then he betrayed me," Glendon said. "I didn't get the stone or, apparently, the queen."

Casek pleaded with his son. "It isn't true."

"I don't believe you. You're nothing but a liar and a disgrace to the crown. By the devil, you had an affair with a witch!" Maeron reached Glendon and stopped to look over his shoulder at his father. "And you allowed that witch to bear an illegitimate child—a dhampir no less."

Glendon laughed. "Is that true? And did you have to kill your own child? Oh, the cruel irony."

I said nothing. It seemed smarter to remain silent.

Disappointment marred Maeron's chiseled features. "All this time, the rumors were true. The two of you conspired to murder my mother."

"He's lying," Casek insisted. "I never intended to go through with it, I swear. I only wanted the fighting to stop. Our people had suffered enough."

"She was a menace to society," Glendon said. He shot an aggrieved look at Britannia. "You were, my dear. Blood-thirsty and aggressive. We were both glad to be rid of you."

Casek faced her. "It was a ruse. I planned for one of my summoners to send you safely through a portal until after the treaty was signed. Then I fully intended to bring you back. I didn't tell you because I knew you'd object. You always wanted to fight."

"Why didn't you bring her back if that was your intention?" Maeron demanded.

I winced. "Because he couldn't. The summoner was killed during the battle."

My father nodded. "I spent years afterward trying to find her on my own so I could bring her back."

"But you couldn't hire summoners to search for her or everyone would know what you did," I finished for him. "And there was a risk they might not believe you." I looked at Britannia. "That *she* might not believe you."

My father hung his head. "I convinced myself that she was dead in order to move on."

Britannia maneuvered through the throng of bodies on the ground and positioned herself between the two kings. "I forgive you, husband."

Maeron blinked at her. "You do?"

She met her son's gaze. "Ours wasn't a happy marriage and, your father's right, I was blinded by ambition. He had no reason to try to protect me, yet he did."

Davina stretched out her hand. "Maeron, don't listen to that twat. We're your family and we love you. Come stand with us."

Glendon smiled at Maeron's hesitation. "That's right, son. Join the winning team. Soon we'll rule the entire realm. With a vampire like you by my side, we'll be invincible as well as immortal."

Britannia's hands cemented to her hips. "Do you honestly believe any son of mine would stand by your side?"

Maeron surprised us all by advancing toward Glendon. The Scottish king's smile broadened with each step.

A growl escaped from Callan. "That's enough, brother."

"You're right. I've had quite enough." Maeron swiveled toward Glendon and bowed his head. "I am at your service, Your Majesty."

Callan's hands clenched into fists. My father's skin turned slightly green.

"Name a place you'd like to keep in that wretched waste-land you call home," Glendon said.

"I quite like Alnwick Castle."

I resisted a glance at Callan. The choice was clearly designed to hurt him.

Glendon clapped his shoulder. "Consider it yours."

Maeron raised his head to look Glendon in the eye and that was when I saw it. A flash of hatred so deep and so powerful that it could have leveled all ten supervolcanoes.

Metal glinted and a dagger appeared in Maeron's hand. He thrust the blade above the fanny pack and straight into the fleshy part of Glendon's abdomen.

Or what should have been the fleshy part.

It took a moment for me to realize that the blade met resistance. Glendon grabbed Maeron by the face and squeezed.

"No!" Davina attempted to rush to her brother's aid, but Callan grabbed her arm and held her in place.

"Now I know where you stand," Glendon said through clenched teeth. "I'm going to break every bone in your body and let your mother watch you die a slow, painful death."

"Father, that's enough," Callan demanded.

"I don't take orders from traitors," Glendon said. "I don't take orders from anyone."

"Where is he getting that strength?" Davina whispered.

I had a hunch that certain witches and wizards on his payroll might have contributed to the king's newfound powers.

An arrow whizzed past me toward Glendon. He snatched the arrow out of the air with his free hand and crushed it. Pieces of metal fell to the ground.

"Shit," Davina said.

No kidding.

I couldn't let him kill Maeron. The vampire was a power-hungry prince with questionable priorities, but he was still my brother. He didn't deserve to have his skull crushed.

I connected to my magic and felt the satisfying click of the key in the lock. I'd used a lot of magic today, more than I ever had in a single span of time. The balance was off. I had to be careful or I could hurt more than my intended target.

Glendon pressed harder and forced Maeron to his knees.

I raised my hand and *pushed*. Glendon skidded backward and released his grip on the prince. Maeron collapsed on the ground in a heap. His moans sent shivers down my spine.

Davina ran to him.

Casek bared his fangs and charged.

Glendon raised a hand and blew my father off his feet. It seemed he'd been imbued with all sorts of powers.

Glendon's laughter rang out. "Thought you could beat me, did you?"

"Your staff's been busy," I said.

Britannia lifted her son off the ground like he weighed no more than a leaf and carried him away.

The ring of fire dissipated and a fresh wave of vampires arrived behind Glendon. He simply pointed and they surged toward us.

The pressure of my magic continued to build. It had never felt this intense before. Usually the release of magic helped me maintain a balance and relieved the pressure.

I'd been using too much.

I had no choice, though. Without it, we didn't have a chance of defeating him. A voice in the back of my mind warned me to slow down, to pull back. That if I continued down this path, I'd be the nuclear explosion I always feared.

I'd kill the enemy, yes, but I'd also take myself and everyone I loved with me.

There would be no winners.

Callan seemed to sense something wasn't right. He observed me with concern as he twisted the neck of an attacking vampire. "Take it easy. You don't want this to be your Birmingham."

I elbowed the vampire behind me in the throat and spun around to finish him off with my axe. The blade severed his head from his body and I barely noticed the blood that now mingled with my own.

"If I slow down, we lose."

He snarled. "You've got silver seeping out of you. If you don't slow down, I lose you."

If I was going to blow anyway, I might as well make it count.

"I need you to do something for me right now." I looked into his green eyes. "Get everyone as far away from here as you can. I don't care if Glendon's guys chase you. Let them."

He stared at me intently. "What are you going to do?"

My breathing hitched. "Just go. Don't come back until the coast is clear." Depending on how things panned out, there may or may not be a stone waiting for him.

"How will I know when the coast is clear?"

I gave him a pointed look. "You'll know."

Britannia smacked his arm. "You heard the knight. Everybody out."

He kissed me hard on the lips. "Come back to me, London."

I offered a weak smile. "No, you come back to me, remember? That's the plan."

I turned away and sprinted toward the king. Behind me, Britannia's voice sounded above all the others. She was a natural commander. A force to be reckoned with. I was glad she was on our team.

Glendon saw an opportunity and hurried toward the safety of the building. I'd go in after him if I had to, but my plan would be more effective outside. My mother would never forgive me for destroying a historical building.

I accessed my air magic and let the wind carry me as high as I could go. I didn't need to reach the clouds.

My skin no longer seeped silver. It glowed. My magic was on the verge of bubbling over.

I set my sights on Glendon, still running. Target acquired.

"Glendon, you dropped the stone!" I yelled from my place in the air.

Instinctively the king stopped and turned.

Magic exploded.

In that moment, I was as close to a sun as anything in this atmosphere could be. A bright star with a black hole of bottomless power at its core. Energy spilled from me in shockwaves. The silver light blinded me and I felt myself losing control. It was too much.

I arced toward the ground like a falling star. If you made a wish on yourself, would it come true?

I'd never know.

I crashed to earth, pain infiltrating my every pore. I saw my mother's smiling face and relief swept over me.

Then the black hole expanded and took me with it.

17

Polly met me at the entrance to the bathroom with a set of folded towels, a sponge, and an oversized bar of soap. I tried not to take offense.

"You made it."

I managed a smile. "I'm not convinced. The fact that there's a bath waiting for me suggests this might be heaven."

She chuckled and used her elbow to open the door. "I can grab a suture kit if you like. You look like you might need fixing."

I glanced at her. "Suture kit? Is there anything you can't do?"

"I started as a seamstress and worked my way up, so no."

"It won't be necessary, but thank you." I accepted the proffered items and entered the bathroom.

"Is it your vampire side that heals quickly?"

I set the pile on the table beside the tub and looked at her. "There are no sides. There's just me."

She gave a crisp nod and reached for the door handle. "Is it true about Queen Britannia?"

"Yes."

"Is she as fearsome as they say?"

"Find out for yourself. She's downstairs."

Polly's face drained of color. "And you recovered that stone you were after?"

"We did." The only thing left of King Glendon after my supernova routine was the stone itself. It sat on the ground, completely unblemished. The only mark on it was the whorl.

"Give me a shout if you need anything," Polly said. "I'll hover."

"Thank you, but there's really no need. Go tend to the others." They weren't all blessed with my healing abilities.

She closed the door and I waited until I heard a soft click before I stripped off my boots and armor. Pain needled me no matter which way I moved. It would take a little longer to heal this time. No doubt about it.

Bubbles floated on top and my hand skimmed the surface. The water was warm and ready. The scent of rosehip filled my nostrils as I sank into the water. A victorious finish to an impossible quest, respite in a castle, and a luxurious bubble bath. Maybe my first instinct was right. Maybe I was in heaven.

Closing my eyes, I sank deeper and let the warm water soothe my aching muscles. I hoped my friends were receiving the same royal treatment.

I heard the door open. "I'm fine, Polly. There's no need to hover."

"It isn't Polly."

I opened my eyes to see Callan leaning against the door-jamb with his arms folded across his broad chest. Fire ignited in my belly at the sight of him. Clean and refreshed, he looked as though he'd just left a modeling gig instead of a battle between Houses.

Bastard.

The vampire prince sauntered toward the tub with the grace of a jungle cat stalking his prey.

"I saw the way you limped into the castle. Thought you might need a hand."

I was too injured and tired to object. "There are a few spots I can't reach without hurting myself."

Callan kneeled beside the tub and reached for the sponge. "You went through quite a lot of moves today."

"Didn't have much of a choice. It was pull out all the stops or lose. Your father was determined to kill us all." I angled my head to study him. "Any regrets?"

"About my father? None at all. I released him from my heart a long time ago. As you said, he would've killed us all and danced a jig on our bodies afterwards." He dipped the sponge in the soapy water. "Where would you like me to start?"

Our gazed locked and I felt a thousand tiny jolts emanate from my core. I was glad I was already seated because my legs would've melted.

I cleared my throat. "Maybe start with the dirt you can see."

He fished out the sponge and squeezed the excess over my breasts. Then he trailed drops of water along the curve of my neck. I leaned my neck to the side and heard a low, predatory growl.

"If you're hungry, I'm sure there's a bottle of synthetic blood in the kitchen. After all, this is your castle."

His mouth hovered next to my ear. "It isn't blood I crave."

A burst of warm air dusted my neck and I shivered.

"You almost died," he said.

"I'm a knight, remember? That happens a lot in my line

of work." I cupped his chiseled jawline with my hand, trans-ferring a line of bubbles to him. "Besides, you resuscitated me. All's well that ends well."

"It wasn't me."

I frowned. "I thought I heard your voice…"

"You needed blood. Mine wouldn't work, not on you."

"Davina?"

He shook his head. "Your father. He was gravely injured, but he insisted."

I sat up quickly, causing water to splash over the edge. "Could he spare it?"

Callan ran the sponge along my cheek. "He spared it. And he lived. He's already sipping tea and complaining about the temperature like the grumpy old man he truly is."

A wave of relief washed over me. "How is it that I'm supposed to be the powerful one, yet you look as fresh as a daisy?" I inspected his handsome face. "Do you even have a scratch on you?"

"I was very fortunate. Then again, I wasn't the one who exploded like a supernatural supernova."

"In other words, you feel fine."

"I do."

"In that case, are you going to keep standing there eyeballing me or are you going to join me?"

With preternatural speed, Callan stripped off his clothes and climbed into the tub. Water spilled over the sides, soaking the floor.

"You might want to be careful of water damage," I said. "Those wooden floorboards have survived centuries. You don't want to sacrifice them for the sake of a frisky bath."

He fixed me with a penetrating stare and leaned forward. "It's hardly a sacrifice."

His mouth fastened on mine, which worked out well for me because I lost the power of speech anyway.

I also lost the power to breathe.

Forgetting my injuries, I lost all track of time. Limbs tangled and bodies joined. Flesh pressed against flesh until I couldn't tell where the dhampir began and the vampire ended. In this moment, only two people existed in the world and they were right here in this clawfoot tub.

By the time we finished, there was almost no water left in the tub and I'd lost control of my muscles too.

Worth it.

Callan shifted so that our bodies were side-by-side in the tub. "You were far more alert than I expected. I thought I'd spend at least a day nursing you back to health."

I shifted my head to look at him. "I'm sorry to disappoint you."

Callan dipped his head and kissed me. "From the moment I met you, you've done nothing but exceed my expectations."

"Ditto."

He reached for a towel. "Would you like me to dry you off now? I might have neglected to mention this is a full-service castle."

I licked my lips. "When you say full-service...?"

His gaze lowered to my naked body, dripping with a mixture of bathwater and sweat.

"I appear to have missed a few spots," he said. "Is it cats that clean themselves by licking?"

I took the towel from his hands and chucked it on the floor. "It isn't limited to cats."

A slow, lascivious smile spread across his face. "I'm glad to hear it. Why should they have all the fun?"

.   .   .

ORKNEY WAS as dramatic and beautiful as I remembered it. The rugged coastline. The fresh air. The tall sandstone cliffs. It wasn't hard to recreate my journey to the site of the original Friseal's Temple. Each step was like remembering the notes to a song.

"This really is the end of the world," Kami said, walking beside me.

"That's why we decided to bring the stones here to destroy them. We're as far from civilization as we can get."

"Are you sure we should destroy them? Maybe we should just store them in your holiday home. Save them for a rainy day."

I peered at her. "They're not pocket money. They're the most powerful stones in the world."

She shrugged. "All the more reason to keep them. You never know when a monster's going to show up from South America and wreak havoc."

"I'm going to pretend you didn't just say that."

I continued walking, aware of the line of supernaturals following in my footsteps. After much deliberation, we decided to destroy the stones employing the same method that was used to create them—by joining forces.

Britannia fell in step beside me. "I thought I'd take a moment to thank you while everyone else is huffing and puffing like they've never walked miles before."

"I'm the one who should be thanking you. You were invaluable."

She smiled. "I always excelled in battle."

I was almost afraid to ask my next question in case I didn't like the response. "What will you do after this?"

"Well, first I'll need to reassure poor Imogen that I have no desire to oust her. Poor lamb must be quaking in her stilettos."

I laughed at the thought of Imogen downing copious amounts of wine in anticipation of the former queen's arrival.

"Then I'll be starting over. Your sister has asked me to teach her a few moves." She cast a glance over her shoulder at Davina. "I think I might enjoy that. She's a lovely girl. Full of potential, like I was once upon a time."

"You're immortal, remember? You still are."

We continued in companionable silence toward our destination. The five stones were currently wrapped in anti-magic chains and stowed in a warded chest. Every so often I glanced over my shoulder to make sure the chest was still part of the entourage. Nicolette Dumont from the West End Werewolf Pack carried one handle and Maeron carried the other. However unlikely we'd be intercepted, the future was forever uncertain and I resolved to remain vigilant until the deed was done.

"Are we there yet?" Minka asked.

Kami pivoted to face her. "You can't be serious. You're in an unspoiled remote location."

"Exactly."

Kami shook her head. "Try to enjoy it."

We arrived at the waterfall and I listened to the admiring noises made by my companions.

"I've never seen any place like this," Briar said. She kneeled by the pool and glided a hand through the water.

"It's pretty special."

"I guess that's why our ancestors chose it," Yardley said. He broke the ward on the chest and opened it. "Let's get to work."

We kept the stones wrapped in chains so that we weren't unduly influenced by their powers. The last thing we needed was someone suddenly reading minds or transforming against their will. We needed this ritual to go smoothly.

"Word to the wise," I said. "Don't knock the stones in the pool or they might end up somewhere else."

Kami peered at the water. "It's a portal?"

"It was for me. I say we take no chances."

We set the five stones in a heap and Minka drew a chalk circle around them. "What if the spell isn't strong enough?"

Ione patted her shoulder. "Have a little faith in yourself, Minka. You're an excellent spell caster."

"And we trust you," Neera added.

"Should we all be part of the circle or should some of us wait outside?" Stevie asked.

Davina stepped on the line of chalk. "I don't care who else is in, but I'm part of it."

"London and I discussed it," Minka began, "and we believe that since we're all watered down versions of the original participants, the more of us that join, the better our chances of accomplishing our goal."

Davina's gaze traveled around the gathered group. "Makes sense."

We formed a circle around the stones and left no one out. Vampire, wizard, witch, werewolf, and fae. All the bloodlines involved in the creation of the stones were represented. I stood in for fae, but it was entirely possible there were others in the group with traces of fae blood as well.

"Now," Minka said.

We each cut a palm and dripped our blood onto the chalk circle until it formed a closed loop. Naturally the vampires used their fangs to puncture the skin. The moment the ends of the circle met, I felt a surge of power and the circle flashed with golden light.

Laughter erupted from the circle. I looked at Neera

across from me and joined the laughter. The earth witch's hair was standing straight on end. Everyone's was. We looked ridiculous.

Minka started to chant, reminding us of our more serious purpose. Our voices mingled with hers in perfect harmony until we seemed to create a single note.

The ground rumbled and the air grew close. In the center of the circle, the stones trembled. Stevie tightened her grip on my hand. This was it. If we failed now...It didn't bear thinking about.

The chanting grew louder. The earth shook harder. The stones resisted their fate.

I *pushed*.

I poured every ounce of magic into the spell.

One of the stones split down the middle. Progress.

The sound reached a fever pitch.

Light flashed, illuminating the entire area. If you didn't know any better, you might mistake it for sunlight. The moment seemed to play out in slow motion. I could see the brown bark on the trees and the blue of the water. In the distance, I glimpsed a hint of the North Sea. Bathed in light, the world was more stunning than I could've imagined.

The next explosion of light forced my eyes closed. I turned away to escape the intensity, but made sure to keep my hands entwined with Davina and Stevie. I couldn't risk breaking the circle.

Another sound pierced the air, so powerful that it seemed to reverberate inside me. It was as though the earth itself was splitting open. The noise ended abruptly and I dared to open my eyes.

A crater had taken the place of the circle. The stones were gone.

The air returned to normal, as did our hair. We released each other's hands and stared.

Yardley was the first to speak. "Bravo. We did it."

I looked around for signs of anything strange. I flipped my hands back and forth and examined my skin. I felt the same, not that I expected to be changed by the spell. It was only the stones that were destroyed rather than the magic connected to them.

Kami banged the heel of her palm against the side of her head. "Anyone else have ringing ears?"

"I'm sure it'll stop in a minute," I said.

Davina peered over the rim of the crater. "That was intense."

Part of me was relieved, yet another part of me felt a pang of loss. *This is why we can't have nice things.*

Kami seemed to sense my mixed feelings. She put a hand on my shoulder and said, "Don't feel bad. This was the only option. You were right, as always."

"Not always." I turned to face her. "I was wrong to lie about so much for so long. I thought I was protecting everyone else, but I was mainly protecting myself."

Kami looked me in the eye. "You're still my best friend. I don't care if you summon a thousand Trios from the fiery pits of the underworld. We all make mistakes."

"Hey, I didn't summon Trio. I found her in the tunnels of one of the underground stations."

"Yeah, I remember the story you gave us."

"I wasn't lying then," I insisted.

She laughed. "You're making this too easy."

Yardley approached us. "I must confess, I wasn't certain our plan would work. I'm pleasantly surprised."

"Thank you for coming," I said. "I know it was a long

way." I also knew he would've preferred to use the stones for his own purposes. The sun would have to wait.

He smiled. "It was an honor to join you. Thank you for entrusting me with the opportunity."

"I suppose you'll be continuing your own quest."

He nodded. "Absolutely. If there's a way to bring back the sun, the People in Support of Ra will find it."

I clapped him on the shoulder. "Good luck, Yardley."

"We should meet for tea next week. Same place as before?"

"Sounds like a plan."

Smiling, the wizard disappeared.

"Teleportation is much cooler than what I can do," Minka complained.

I looked at her, incredulous. "You crafted a spell that helped destroy five ancient and powerful stones. It's the stuff of gods, Minka."

She pursed her lips. "I guess that's cool, too."

Kami knocked her with an elbow. "That's it. We're forcing you outside your comfort zone on a regular basis from now on."

"I can't. Someone has to be in charge of the paperwork."

"Then we'll draft a schedule where everyone takes a turn playing bureaucrat," Kami said. "We're going to help you become the favorite version of yourself."

Minka scrunched her nose. "I thought it's supposed to be the best version of myself."

"I'd choose favorite. That gives us a little leeway for fun and games. Best is too much pressure."

Minka seemed to take the advice on board, which was a feat in and of itself.

"Do you want to sit together on the train back to the city?" Stevie asked Kami.

"I'm not going straight back," Kami said. "I'm taking a little detour through Morpeth."

I smiled at her. "That sounds like a great idea. Take lots of photos."

"I fully intend to. I'll send you one of me in the beer garden. I might even be sober when I do it."

We gathered together and prepared to depart the archipelago. Deep in the shadows, something stirred. The creature didn't set off any alarms, so I watched to see whether our guest would reveal itself. It seemed to be moving in the opposite direction. As it ambled away, I discerned the faint silhouette of a giant tortoise shell.

Ione followed my gaze. "What is it, London?"

I smiled. "Nothing. Just a shadow."

18

I tiptoed up the steps to my flat with the menagerie in tow. I'd originally chosen the top floor so I had access to the rooftop, but the location made it challenging to sneak the menagerie in and out of the building. Now that the danger had passed, hopefully the animals could stay put. I didn't need an eviction notice after everything I'd just been through.

I ushered them into the flat and hurriedly closed the door behind me. Despite my stern warning, Herman continued to bleat. If any neighbors claimed to see or hear anything, I'd feign ignorance. It was the one instance where I approved of gaslighting.

Once we were safely in the flat, the animals seemed reluctant to leave my side. Poor things were traumatized by all the recent relocations. I could tell from the wet patch of fur that Big Red had been gnawing on his paw.

Jemima immediately started pecking the sofa. Hera hissed at Sandy when the fox tried to settle beside the cat on the sofa cushion. We'd never be one big, happy family, but was there truly any such thing? All families, whether by birth or choice, came with their fair share of problems.

Herman trotted into the kitchen ahead of me. The pygmy goat was always ready for his next meal. Big Red attached himself to my foot, forcing me to walk to the kitchen like a zombie to prepare their meals.

Generally speaking, it was a typical day in Britannia City and I was grateful for it.

Once they'd eaten, I focused on my own meal. No surprise the cupboard was bare. I'd need to hit the shops now that I was finally home. In the meantime, I inhaled a bowl of vegetable soup. As I placed the empty bowl in the sink, I heard a tapping noise and ventured into the living room to investigate. The animals surrounded the window in a semi-circle.

"Is it Barnaby?" I expected the raven would turn up sooner or later. He always did.

I pulled aside the curtain and was pleasantly surprised to see Callan on the balcony.

I opened the window. "You know you don't have to sneak around anymore, right?"

He climbed into the flat. "I've become rather fond of the unorthodox entrance."

"The coronation is tomorrow. Shouldn't you be heading up to Scotland?" I dusted off his shoulders. "You look pretty good for a vampire king."

He kissed my cheek. "A backhanded compliment. How sweet." He slid a hand into his pocket. "I come bearing gifts."

I closed my eyes. "Lay it on me."

"Why did you close your eyes?"

"If it's a gift horse, I don't think I'm supposed to look it in the mouth."

He chuckled. "Open your eyes. It isn't a horse." He

opened his palm to reveal a small, purple fruit. "Becoming king has its advantages."

I stared at the plum, unable to speak.

Callan grinned. "I've rendered you speechless. My work here is done."

I took the plum and inhaled its scent. "You remembered."

"How could I forget one of your most treasured memories of your mother?"

"Thank you. You have no idea what this means to me."

"I do, which is exactly why I'm giving it to you. Feel free to eat this one instead of treating it like a keepsake. There are more where that came from."

I tucked the plum in my pocket. "Later. I don't want to talk to you with plum juice dripping down my chin. It isn't sexy."

He tucked a strand of my hair behind my ear. "Everything you do is sexy, London."

"Is that the sound of a gauntlet being thrown? Because I'm pretty sure I can rise to the challenge."

He bent his head and kissed me.

Herman bleated, interrupting the moment. I turned to look at the goat. "Keep it up and you'll find yourself at the market, buddy."

Herman lowered his head and trotted over to sit on the floor by the sofa.

"Would you mind if I practiced my speech on you?" Callan asked.

"Are you sure? I'm not exactly your target audience."

"No, but you're the most important one."

"Is there time for popcorn?"

"No."

"Okay. Let me get comfortable first."

I retreated to the sofa and the menagerie immediately crowded around me. Big Red settled on my lap and I stroked the red panda's fur as Callan took his place in front of us.

He adopted a regal stance, which seemed to come naturally to him. "Thank you to everyone for welcoming me back. As I'm sure you can imagine, I've missed the mountains and glens, as well as the forests and moorlands that were my childhood home. I'm fortunate to return to a thriving country. Others haven't fared as well. As you know, I was responsible for destruction in the city of Birmingham twenty years ago. The residents have suffered immeasurable loss and we've been slow to make amends. Too slow. With our deepest apologies, I'd like to announce that House Duncan will be matching the reparation efforts of House Lewis and we hope to one day soon see Birmingham thrive as it deserves."

I burst into applause, scaring Big Red off my lap.

"My next act as king, in partnership with House Lewis, is to announce the introduction of a synthetic blood product to replace our use of human blood. This product has been tried and tested by a talented team of vampires, and we've determined the product will serve as a suitable substitute. To that end, I am dissolving tribute centers throughout the land. There will be no more requirements for human blood."

I drew a steadying breath. A bold choice, but one I knew he'd been preparing for, even before we met.

I continued to listen quietly until I heard, "Magic will no longer be outlawed."

I gasped. "Are you insane?"

He ignored me and kept talking. "When we make magic forbidden, we deny some of our subjects the right to be who they truly are. We suppress them and oppress them. That's not the kind of leader I wish to be. If we have to rule by fear, then we don't deserve to rule at all."

I picked up my jaw off the floor and let him continue.

"And my final act today is to repeal the law regarding dhampirs."

I met his gaze and he offered a small smile.

"If you are the child born of a vampire and another species...If you are a vampire or witch carrying a dhampir baby, you have nothing to fear from House Duncan." He cleared his throat. "And I have it on good authority that House Lewis will be making a similar announcement soon."

I imagined the vampire spectators would be mildly confused by the proclamation. Only time would tell.

"And now allow me to introduce my consort, London Hayes of the Knights of Boudica." He extended his hand toward me.

I shook my head. "I won't be there, remember? You're going tomorrow."

"Not without you."

I expelled a breath. "Callan, we've talked about this. I'm a dhampir. You're the new king of the north. You can't have someone like me at your side. New law or not, it'll upset your subjects. They need time to adjust to the changes."

He scooted the animals aside and joined me on the sofa, clasping my hand. "I've given it a lot of thought and, the truth is, if I can't have you by my side, then I don't want it."

I stared at him. "Callan, that's absurd."

He ran his thumb along my hand. "Listen to me, London. We have to be the change we want to see in the world. It starts with us. Today." He grinned. "More specifi-cally, tomorrow."

In my head, I heard my mother's voice repeating similar

words. *We must be the change we wish to see in the world, London. What we fail to change, we are doomed to repeat.*

I squeezed his hand. "You're right. I just don't want to put you in a difficult position."

"Life is filled with difficult positions. It's how we handle them that defines who we are."

I nodded. "I know who I am now." And I wasn't afraid to embrace her—not anymore. "All right. I'll come with you."

The menagerie seemed to understand my decision and grunted their displeasure.

Callan looked at them and smiled. "Don't worry. I'll have a special carriage prepared for them. You won't have to leave them behind again." He kissed my forehead. "I'll collect you tomorrow at eight."

"I'll be ready."

He transformed into a butterfly and fluttered out the window. I followed behind, climbing onto the balcony to watch him leave. It seemed incredible there was a time when the sight of a butterfly would knot every muscle in my body. Now, as I watched this particular butterfly blend with the night, I felt something else entirely.

Hope.

It wasn't a perfect world, but it was ours and we'd keep striving to improve it—one stone at a time.

GREAT NEWS, readers! This isn't the last story set in the Midnight Empire world. Read on for the first chapter of Endless Knight, Midnight Empire: The Restoration, Book 1.

To receive updates on upcoming books and sales, sign up for my newsletter by visiting my website at www. annabelchase.com.

SNEAK PREVIEW

I sat on a ledge with my legs dangling over the side of a red brick building. If I didn't have a job to do, I'd take time to enjoy the quiet of the neighborhood. Hudson Square was one of the least populated areas in the city, which meant fewer lights and less foot traffic. It wasn't always like this. According to royal records, it was once a hub for large media companies. The blocks heaved with luxury high-rise buildings and glass monuments to technology. When the neighborhood's fortunes rose, it became a sought-after location close to the Hudson River.

When the neighborhood's fortunes fell, they fell hard.

The simultaneous eruption of ten of the world's supervolcanoes resulted in enough ash in the atmosphere to block the sun. The Eternal Night wasn't the only outcome.

When darkness fell, the monsters came.

Deep in the earth's core, they bided their time until ten doors opened and allowed them entry. By land, sea, and air they attacked and invaded. Active calderas in the Americas and Australasia meant those areas suffered more than other continents. The entire continent of South America succumbed to the magma and monsters. Here in Hudson Square, they managed to wipe out most of the skyscrapers and destroy half the neighborhood before the vampires were able to secure it. Its proximity to the Hudson River became a negative feature. The damage was psychological as well as physical. Residents circumvented this neighborhood even after all these years, which was the reason House August refused to invest in its restoration. A shame, really. The place had potential.

I leaned over the ledge. There were five stories between my feet and the pavement. Thankfully I didn't mind heights. Sometimes I fantasized that a mighty dragon would breach the city wards and whisk me away. When I was feeling particularly lonely, the dragon would turn out to be a hot dragon shifter who fell madly in love with me. Too bad dragon shifters didn't exist.

I kept my eye on the defunct Big Apple tour bus parked on the street below. My boss hated when anybody referred to the city as 'the Big Apple,' which only encouraged me to do it as frequently as possible. As the Director of Security for House August, Olis had a lot of responsibility and the wizard didn't suffer fools gladly.

In other words, he was a joy to torment.

Bored, I scraped the dirty heels of my boots against the brick. I would've preferred to drop down and confront the occupants of the bus right now. Get the confrontation over with. I knew I couldn't do that, though. My recklessness was the reason I was here in the first place, working for House August as an indentured servant in their security division. Thanks to my actions, I'd been given a choice—a public beheading in Times Square or servitude. I chose the latter. I wasn't big on spectacles unless I was the one in charge of it. Now the royal vampires owned me. I was their tool.

Arguably a tool was better than a weapon, which had been my life before this one. 'Death Bringer' they called me, among other things. The moniker was a little on the nose for my taste, but it conveyed the right message. I was both feared and revered by vampires because of my rare type of magic.

I rubbed an apple on my chest and bit into it. One of the perks of my position was decent food. No need to scavenge or starve. House August owned magical orchards and vineyards on Long Island. Unlike me, those witches and wizards were compensated for their work. If I'd been a regular witch, maybe they would've offered me a cushy job like that —help them grow their blueberries and blackberries or tend to the grapes that made the wine.

Sadly I wasn't that kind of witch. My magic had limited uses, most of which involved death.

I watched with interest as a rat emerged from a nearby dumpster and scrambled toward the bus. Rats had been a real problem in the city in the early years of the Eternal Night. They'd once been as small as cats, but the changing environment created fertile ground for their evolution. When House August seized control of the city, one of their first acts was to deal with the growing rat population. It wasn't as altruistic as it sounded. The rats were spreading disease among the human population and the vampires needed human blood to survive, which made rats Public Enemy Number One.

The rat headed straight for the bus and I suspected it sensed food inside. From my vantage point, I could see the dumpster was empty. I gave House August credit—the royal family was serious about sanitation.

The rat scampered toward the bus and stopped short about a foot from the bus's exterior. I watched carefully.

"Come on, buddy. Don't give up yet. One more try," I said under my breath.

The rat started forward but only made it an inch before it bounced backward.

"And that's a wrap, folks," I said to no one in particular.

I finished the apple and threw the core to the back of the alley. I had a good arm. The security team even tried to recruit me for the House softball team, but Olis refused permission. Only employees were allowed to play under the stadium lights, not indentured servants. Their loss.

The rat turned and lumbered toward its snack.

In the distance I spotted movement. A rabble of butterflies meant vampire patrol. I recognized the orange and black colors of Doug's team and checked my watch. Yep. Right on schedule.

Most people broke into an anxiety rash when they noticed a cluster of butterflies headed in their direction. Not me. I knew most of the vampires in the city, at least the ones with the ability to transform into butterflies. House August was smart enough to employ any vampire with advanced abilities, which was probably one of the reasons the royal family had managed to amass so much power. And even if I didn't recognize a particular vampire, there was a decent chance they'd recognize me.

The bus rocked once from side to side. Blue light flashed around it.

Time to go.

I retrieved a pocket knife from my utility belt and waited for the air to grow still. No sense letting a breeze thwart my plan. I sliced my palm and let three drops of blood fall to the pavement just outside the bus.

That ought to do the trick.

I watched the tiny sparks with satisfaction. They must've

decided the ancient bus was a decent hiding spot and they didn't need a stronger ward.

They'd be wrong.

I hooked a bungee cord to the ledge and shimmied down the side of the building. The lack of light in this neighborhood would make my entrance easier.

When I reached the second floor, I released the cord and jumped. My boots hit the top of the bus with a thud. Not quite the nimble landing I intended. From there I jumped to the pavement.

The door jerked open and a head popped out to investigate the sound. I grabbed him by the neck and slammed him against the side of the bus, squeezing hard. "I could've sworn I heard somebody speaking Latin in there. Know anything about that?"

He struggled to speak but no words came out. No surprise since I was pressing on his windpipe.

"Inquisitor," somebody yelled from inside the bus.

"Tell your buddies I'm not an inquisitor." I noticed the man's bulging eyes. "Hold on. I can see you're busy. I'll tell them." Still gripping his neck, I poked my head inside the open door. "Hey, guys. Just FYI, I'm not an inquisitor."

Another man ran to the door. Visible blue veins and a bright red scar made his face look like a topographical map featuring a river of blood.

Scarface shook a fist at me. "May the sun make you perish!"

"Ooh, burn. The ultimate insult. If I were a vampire, I'd be deeply offended."

"You're a disgrace to your kind."

"Takes one to know one." Very mature, I realized, but it was the first comeback that came to mind. "What are you guys doing in there? I saw blue light so unless you're having a special sale…"

Fingers dug into my hand and I released my grip on the man's neck. I wasn't trying to kill him, although I was sure he didn't see it that way.

I grabbed him by the collar and dragged him inside the bus. There were four men total and evidence of magic everywhere. Wizards. A redhead attempted to clear the contraband from view.

"Don't bother, Clifford. I've already seen it."

The redhead frowned. "Clifford?"

"The Big Red Dog?" I made a noise of exasperation. "Did no one here read children's books? No wonder you turned to a life of crime."

"If you're not an inquisitor, then why do you care if we use magic?" my former chokehold victim asked.

"I work for House August and your little activities here are considered a security threat."

"You're one of us. How can you work for them?" Clifford asked.

"First, I'm not one of you. Second, we all do what we have to do to survive."

"If that's what you believe, then you should let us go," the curly-haired wizard said. "We're only trying to do the same." He wore wire-rimmed spectacles and a T-shirt bearing an image of the Statue of Liberty. Instead of a torch, she held a wand.

"No, you're trying to use magic for your own selfish purposes, which is illegal."

"It isn't selfish to want to feed our families," Clifford said. "This is the only avenue available to us."

"You're lucky I'm the one finding you. Anybody else

would've dragged the four of you into Times Square for a beheading and made a public spectacle of your deaths."

The curly-haired wizard eyed me carefully. "You're not going to do that?"

"No."

"Why not?" Scarface asked.

"Because I'm in a good mood and I've decided to let you off with a warning."

"You have the authority to do that?" the redhead asked.

I tapped my chin. "Let me think. Are you going to tell anyone?"

Clifford shook his head. "Not me. Why are you in a good mood?"

"Aw, I'm so glad you asked. You see, I have it on good authority that the taco truck on Eighth Avenue is getting a shipment of avocados this week. Do you know what that means?"

They shook their heads.

I clapped my hands. "Guacamole, people. Come on."

It was the little things that made life worth living. It had been at least a year since my last taste of guacamole and that was only because I'd worked security for the king and queen's anniversary party at the royal compound and snuck as many guacamole-laden nibbles as I could manage without getting caught.

"I'm allergic to avocado," Clifford said.

I rolled my eyes. "Of course you are."

"Why were you watching us if you didn't know what we were doing?" Scarface asked.

"I was made aware of an illegal shipment of mint to Battery Park and traced one of the larger deliveries to this bus."

Scarface elbowed Clifford in the gut. "I told you not to purchase so much of it at once. Small transactions only."

"I've been waiting for a couple days for something to happen and finally it did." I clapped my hands once in dramatic fashion. "Let there be blue light!"

"We're not hurting anybody," Scarface complained.

"You're hurting the system. Magic is against the law unless you have special dispensation like me. Latin is forbidden. Mint is for vampires only. End of story."

"Vampires only outlawed magic because they know that witches and wizards would be able to overthrow them with it," Clifford said.

Arms crossed, I looked down my nose at him. "And what magic spell would be powerful enough to eradicate vampire rule? I'd love to know."

I turned to look at the fourth wizard who'd been silent this whole time and it was then that I saw it.

The makings of a magical bomb.

My stomach lurched. These wizards weren't simply buying mint for healing tonics or their tea. I'd bet good money they were the wizards responsible for the subway bombing last month. Witnesses described a flash of blue light before the station blew up.

My gaze shifted from the bomb to Scarface. Our eyes locked and I saw the glimmer of recognition in his eyes.

"Displodo!" he yelled.

A snapping sound followed.

The four wizards shot out of the bus like their clothes were on fire. It took me a second but I got there in the end. A magical bomb was about to explode two feet away from me.

Terrific.

Blue light flashed in waves and I felt my body fly sideways and slam against a hard surface. Metal creaked and groaned. I toppled outside and landed on the pavement flat on my stomach. The inside of my mouth tasted like blood and my one eye didn't seem to want to open. Pain bloomed on the side of my head.

Those slimy bastards. I should've rounded them up and presented them to Olis on a platter. Freakin' Clifford. I bet the only thing big about him was his cowardice.

I gave myself a minute to recover from the blast. The bus was in pieces around me. No doubt all evidence of magic was gone. I'd have to track the four wizards from scratch.

I heard the crunch of metal as someone slowly and methodically made their way toward me. A Good Samaritan, mayhap? Unlikely. We didn't have many of those in the city. It was everyone for themselves. Only vampires could afford to be magnanimous, not that it was in their nature. In my experience, they were inherently selfish creatures.

I lifted my chin off the ground and looked directly at a pair of familiar black boots. They were distinctive in that they bore the triquetra on each tongue. I only knew this because I'd been forced to scrub them on multiple occasions after incidents that may or may not have been my fault.

I turned my head sideways and peered up at my boss. "Hey, Olis."

The wizard regarded me from beneath a line of judgmental peach fuzz that masqueraded as eyebrows. "Back to your usual shenanigans, I see."

I scrambled to my feet. "Mission accomplished, sir."

He waved a hand. "You call this mess an accomplishment?"

"I know what the mint is being used for. That's the important part. Who cares about a teeny tiny explosion?"

"I believe it was Machiavelli who said that the ends

justify the means," Olis replied. "Is that the kind of person you'd like to align yourself with?"

"I work for vampires, sir." I shot an apologetic look at the vampire beside him. "No offense, Bruno."

Bruno shrugged. He was the most lackadaisical vampire I'd ever met, which was probably the reason he ended up on a security team alongside a witch and a wizard.

"Anyway, Machiavelli is widely misunderstood," I continued.

Olis observed me with a mixture of amusement and irritation. "How so?"

"The concept is more complex. It doesn't mean we can do what we want without consequences as long as the outcome is favorable."

"Then what does it mean?" Olis asked.

I sighed. "Read *The Prince* and then *Discourses on Livy* and you'll get a fuller picture."

"How do you know all that?" Bruno asked.

"Because I communicate with his ghost at night."

For a split second, Bruno looked like he might believe me. Then his raised brow morphed into a scowl.

"From books." I patted his chest. "You should visit the library sometime. You might learn why you can't transform into a butterfly like your superior vampire buddies."

Bruno's fangs snapped into place and I laughed.

Olis stepped between us. "Is that wise, Bruno?"

The vampire's nostrils flared. "I'm not afraid of you, Britt the Bloody."

I pointed at him. "That attitude right there proves how desperately you need an education."

Olis grabbed me by the elbow and steered me away before things escalated. "Bruno, pick through the debris and see what you can find," he called over his shoulder.

Good. Let Bruno do the grunt work for a change.

"Do you want me to write up a report on what I found? I think it's connected to the subway bombing last month."

Olis blinked rapidly. "Later. There's a more pressing matter."

I frowned. "More pressing than a magical bomb?"

"Your presence has been requested. That's the reason I'm here."

"Really? I thought you were here to discipline me."

"For what?"

"Nothing," I said quickly. He didn't need to know that I'd intended to let the four escaped wizards go—before I discovered their treachery, of course.

"The queen has asked for you personally."

I looked at him askance. "Queen Dionne?"

"Is there any other?"

"Well, let me think. There's Queen Margot and Queen Iris. Is there a Queen Britannia or did I make that one up?"

He sighed in exasperation. "Is there any other queen who would summon you?"

"Technically, no, although I don't know why Queen Dionne would want to see me. I don't think she knows my name."

I rarely interacted with the queen. With King Maxwell on a business trip and the prince-who-shall-not-be-named holding down the fort in the Southern Territories, Queen Dionne must've had no choice but to summon me herself.

"Clearly she knows it well enough to send for you. Does everything have to be combative with you?"

"The last time I exchanged words with the queen, it was for the king to offer me the choice between death and a life of servitude. Forgive me if I'm not in a hurry to relive that moment."

Olis loosened his grip on my elbow. "I'm sure whatever the queen has in store for you—it isn't death."

Fear gathered at the base of my tongue and I swallowed. "I've never known you to be wrong, Olis. Do me a favor and don't start now."

You can read the rest of the story here: Endless Knight, Midnight Empire: The Restoration, Book 1.

ALSO BY ANNABEL CHASE

Printed in Great Britain
by Amazon